He'd very nearly given in to temptation and kissed Sophie.

What was more, she would've welcomed his kiss; he'd seen it in her eyes, felt it in the tension-laden air. Griffin prided himself on his discipline and self-control. So what had happened in that moment with Sophie?

The attraction was there, had been there from the first moment she'd walked into his office. He'd managed to tamp it down to an awareness, and she'd hidden the fact, as well. Most of the time, anyway. But that moment in front of the fireplace had shattered their pretense of disinterest.

This was going to complicate things. Big-time. And not just over the next couple of days while they were trapped inside, but over the long term, too.

Now, as Griffin worked his way out to the place where the bridge had collapsed and nearly killed them, he realized he was probably out of luck retrieving their suitcases.

For the duration of the storm, it looked as though he and Sophie were going to be down to borrowed clothes and doused PDAs.

And each other.

JESSICA ANDERSEN

SNOWED IN
with the BOSS

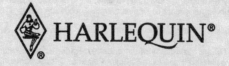

HARLEQUIN®

TORONTO • NEW YORK • LONDON
AMSTERDAM • PARIS • SYDNEY • HAMBURG
STOCKHOLM • ATHENS • TOKYO • MILAN • MADRID
PRAGUE • WARSAW • BUDAPEST • AUCKLAND

Special thanks and acknowledgment to Jessica Andersen for her contribution to the Kenner County Crime Unit miniseries.

Recycling programs
for this product may
not exist in your area.

ISBN-13: 978-0-373-69387-0
ISBN-10:   0-373-69387-7

SNOWED IN WITH THE BOSS

ABOUT THE AUTHOR

Though she's tried out professions ranging from cleaning sea lion cages to cloning glaucoma genes, from patent law to training horses, Jessica is happiest when she's combining all these interests with her first love: writing romances. These days she's delighted to be writing full-time on a farm in rural Connecticut that she shares with a small menagerie and a hero named Brian. She hopes you'll visit her at www.JessicaAndersen.com for info on upcoming books, contests and to say "hi!"

Books by Jessica Andersen

HARLEQUIN INTRIGUE

734—DR. BODYGUARD
762—SECRET WITNESS
793—INTENSIVE CARE
817—BODY SEARCH
833—COVERT M.D.
850—THE SHERIFF'S DAUGHTER
868—BULLSEYE
893—RICOCHET*
911—AT CLOSE RANGE*
928—RAPID FIRE*
945—RED ALERT
964—UNDER THE MICROSCOPE
982—PRESCRIPTION: MAKEOVER
1005—CLASSIFIED BABY
1012—MEET ME AT MIDNIGHT
1036—DOCTOR'S ORDERS
1061—TWIN TARGETS
1068—WITH THE M.D....AT THE ALTAR?
1093—MANHUNT IN THE WILD WEST*
1120—SNOWED IN WITH THE BOSS

*Bear Claw Creek Crime Lab

CAST OF CHARACTERS

Griffin Vaughn—The wealthy technology developer has sworn off women for good. When a blizzard traps him and his pretty new assistant together at his mountain estate, she makes him want to reconsider. But will his former military training be enough to keep them both alive when it becomes clear that they're stranded with a killer?

Sophie LaRue—After spending much of her life caring for her ailing mother, Sophie is just now beginning to live her life. Does she dare trust her handsome boss with her life…and her heart?

Luke Vaughn—Griffin's three-year-old son is safe at home, but his welfare rules Griffin's actions.

Vincent Del Gardo—The mob boss, head of the Del Gardo crime family in Las Vegas, is on the lam after escaping from a courthouse jail. Are the rumors true that he's hiding out in Kenner County?

Nicky Wayne—The head of the rival Wayne crime family wants Del Gardo dead, no matter what it takes…or how many innocent lives are lost in the process.

Perry Long—The contractor Griffin hired to renovate his mountain estate came with excellent references, but there have been too many suspicious delays in the months since. What is he up to?

Sheriff Patrick Martinez—The sheriff of Kenner County is cursing the blizzard that has shut down several important investigations, destroyed crucial evidence and stranded Griffin and Sophie miles from help.

Chapter One

"We'll reach the estate soon," Griffin Vaughn said to his executive assistant, Sophie LaRue, as their rented SUV thundered down the Colorado highway, headed into the mountains.

He was driving; he preferred to drive himself rather than hire limos because he disliked putting his safety in someone else's hands, professional or not. Sophie sat in the passenger seat, her entire attention focused on the breathtaking Colorado scenery. The sweeping vista was shadowed by the distant Rocky Mountains, and the entire scene was overhung by an ominous gray winter sky.

At Griffin's words, she glanced over at him. "I hope so. We need to be done at Lonesome Lake and back down off the mountain before the weather hits."

In her mid-twenties, with wavy, dark blond hair and light brown eyes almost the same color, Sophie was a knockout, hands down. The cinnamon-colored sweater she wore beneath a stylish wool coat accented her undeniable curves, and her neatly tailored pants managed to be simultaneously professional and sexy. Even a cynical, "been there, done that, got the scars to prove it" businessman like Griffin could appreciate the aesthetics. However, that didn't change the fact that she was a dozen years younger than his thirty-nine, and she was his employee, both of which meant she was way off-limits, even if he was looking. Which he wasn't.

Yet he kept feeling the need to fill the silence that stretched between them as the highway unwound beneath the rental's wheels. The fact that he bothered trying to make small talk, which he wouldn't have done with Sophie's middle-aged, über-experienced predecessor, Kathleen, just went to prove what Griffin already knew: he was badly off his game.

He was tired, hungry and irritable. His meeting in New York City had started off bad and had gotten worse the longer he and Sophie stayed, forcing him to pull the plug after only two days of negotiations. He'd decided to return home to San Francisco and see if things went better long-distance, only to have his private jet delayed several hours on the tarmac while air traffic control tried to reroute them around a series of major snowstorms that were blanketing the Midwest.

The frustrations and delays had all added up to Griffin being in an admittedly foul mood by the time they'd finally taken off. That was why, when he'd gotten the voice-mail message that renovations to his Rocky Mountain retreat in the Four Corners region of Colorado had been delayed yet again by another "accident," he'd ordered his private plane to set down near Kenner County. Griffin had suspected for some time that his contractor, Perry Long, was taking him for a ride, and it was past time to deal with it.

The pilot, Hal Jessup, had warned him that there was some serious weather on the way, but Griffin had been adamant. He might not have sewn up VaughnTec's acquisition of the HiTek memory module he was jonesing to get his hands on, but he was going to get *something* done on this trip, damn it. He was going to deal with Perry Long, once and for all. The swindling contractor wasn't going to know what hit him.

Besides, according to the weather forecast, they had a few more hours before the blizzard hit. That should be plenty of time for him and Sophie to drive out to the estate, get a look at the renovations, and then drive back down into Kenner City, where Sophie had already booked them into a decent B and B. She had also arranged for them to meet with Perry the following day, weather permitting. And it damn well better permit as far as Griffin was concerned. He was done with the contractor and his excuses.

"Looks like someone's getting a jump on being stranded in the snow," Sophie said as they rounded a corner and an accident came into view up ahead. Behind a row of cherry-red flares, a battered pickup truck was stuck partway in a ditch off to the side of the road. A police cruiser and tow truck were on-scene, their lights flashing brightly in the gloom. Several men were huddled around the rear of the entrapped vehicle, working on securing a winch to the rear axle.

"Don't let the weathermen talk you into blizzard-induced hysteria," Griffin said. "They're in cahoots with the grocery stores, trying to sell out all the bread, eggs and milk."

She grinned a little and lifted a shoulder. "I'm a California girl. I've never been in a snowstorm before. Until three days ago, I'd never even been on a plane."

Griffin stifled a wince at the reminder of just how green his new executive assistant was. He'd told the retiring Kathleen to find her own replacement—someone efficient with no social life to speak of, who wouldn't mind working the crazy-long hours required by his position as head of VaughnTec. He hadn't bothered reminding Kathleen that his new assistant should be middle-aged and highly experienced, because he'd figured that would've been a given.

Yet Kathleen had hired green, gorgeous Sophie LaRue and disappeared on her retirement cruise. Worse, she had either left her cell phone behind, or she was ignoring his calls, in a blatant signal of "Don't call me, I'll call you." Griffin should know; he was a master with that line. But he'd given up after a while anyway, because what good would it do him now to bark at Kathleen? She'd retired. What happened next was up to him.

He'd been tempted to un-hire Sophie the moment she'd walked through his office door, introduced herself, knocked him for a loop with an instant blast of sexual chemistry, and five minutes later spilled most of a pot of coffee on a stack of important papers. But Kathleen had already shown the new executive assistant the basics of the job, and Griffin was in the middle of delicate negotiations to acquire a memory module that was vital to his newest handheld computer PDA. All of which meant he didn't have the time to interview or train another assistant. Besides, he trusted Kathleen, and figured she must've seen something in Sophie, some reason she thought the two of them would click. Kathleen had always had a knack for reading people, and predicting which employees would work well together. Trusting that even if he didn't see it right off the bat, he'd let his new assistant stay on the job, and they'd both done their best to make it work.

He'd overlooked her occasional bouts of inexperience and nerves, and the clumsiness those nerves seemed to bring out. For her part, she'd worked the long hours without protest, and often took paperwork home with her when she left for the night. And if he'd caught a hint or two that Sophie reciprocated the raw physical attraction he felt for her, they were both doing a fine job of gritting their teeth and ignoring it. They'd been working together nearly a month now, and they'd achieved a functional, if tenuous, boss-and-assistant relationship.

"The cop's waving for us to pull over," she said now as they rolled up to the accident. "I hope your license is good."

"If it's not, I'm blaming it on you," Griffin said, only halfway joking as he stopped the rental and lowered the window.

"Afternoon, folks," the cop said, taking a not-very-casual look from Griffin to Sophie and back. "If you're planning on spending the night in the hotel, you missed the turn by about a mile. Nothing much up this way except pines, rocks and ice." The officer looked to be in his late thirties. He was tall and dark-haired, with vivid blue eyes that were cool and assessing, and didn't look like they missed much.

Griffin saw the edge of a pointed star on the cop's uniform shirt beneath his heavy parka, and made the connection. "Sheriff Martinez?"

The cop's eyes narrowed. "Do I know you?"

"We spoke on the phone when your people needed access to my estate. I'm Griffin Vaughan." Griffin nodded in Sophie's direction. "My assistant, Sophie LaRue." When there was no immediate response from the sheriff of Kenner County, a flutter of long-unused instinct stirred the fine hairs at Griffin's nape. "Do you want to see our IDs?"

Martinez shook his head, and finally relaxed a degree. "No. It's fine. Sorry. Things have been...complicated around here lately. We're giving everyone a second and third look." The sheriff paused. "Are you two headed up to Lonesome Lake?"

Griffin's new estate had been named for the large, spring-fed lake on the property, one of only a few open bodies of water in the immediate area. The lake was located near the main entrance to the sprawling grounds; the driveway cut straight across the middle, running over a sturdy cement-pylon bridge. The promise of summertime fishing, along with a hell of a mountain view, had sold Griffin on the place. The lowball price hadn't hurt, either, though in retrospect it should've been a red flag. Since he'd taken possession of Lonesome Lake, the property had been one long-distance headache after another.

Griffin nodded in answer to the sheriff's question. "Just a quick in-and-out. I gave the live-in couple the month off because of the reno, and the construction crew has undoubtedly gone home to wait out the weather, but I wanted to get a look at the place before we sit down for a meeting with Perry tomorrow."

"You picked a hell of a time to visit." Martinez glanced at the sky. "They're saying this storm could take a couple of days to blow through, maybe more."

"We'll be back down in the city before it starts," Griffin said. "I don't have any desire to be snowed in up there until after the reno is complete." And certainly not with his executive secretary. Lonesome Lake was intended for family, not business.

Griffin had bought the estate to be a getaway for him and his three-year-old son, Luke, and Luke's male nanny, Darryn, both of whom were waiting for him back in San Francisco. The estate was intended to be a luxurious "just the guys" cabin, a place that would let him retreat from the hoopla that came with being a multi-millionaire under the age of forty who made regular appearances on the Steele Most Wealthy list and almost all of San Fran's "Most Eligible Bachelor" roundups.

Those lists invariably included personal tidbits such as his divorce from songwriter Monique Claire, his single father status, and the fact that he'd been a decorated marine technical specialist before taking over struggling VaughnTec and making it into a megacorporation.

Back when Griffin had been in the military, he'd built weapons and tracking tools out of whatever he'd been able to scrounge from the field. As a civilian, he focused more on handheld computers, but the gadget-building theory was the same, and the self-discipline and ruthless logic he'd learned in the battle zones had served him well in the business world.

Unfortunately, his military service only added to his dossier as far as the San Fran socialites were concerned. That, combined with his net worth and dark good looks, had made him the target of too many gold diggers to count. In fact, he'd stopped counting the wannabe Mrs. Vaughns around a year ago, right around the time he'd stopped dating. His lack of interest had only increased the pressure from the gold diggers, which was why he'd bought Lonesome Lake. He needed to get the hell away from his work and the city he'd grown up in, and he wanted someplace comfortable to do it.

Which was great in theory, but so far had been seriously lacking in practice, due to the construction glitches.

Griffin had hired Perry as his general contractor based on the Realtor's recommendation and a handful of local references, and had signed off on a basic updating of the forty year-old structure. At first, the contractor's reports of things needing immediate repair or replacement had seemed reasonable enough. As the months had dragged on, though, and the schedule had doubled, and then tripled, Griffin's patience had decreased in direct proportion to the budget's increase. Now he just wanted to put an end to whatever the hell was going on up at the estate, regardless of whether that meant a sit-down with Perry…or lining up a new contractor.

"We should get moving if we're going to beat the storm," he said pointedly to the sheriff.

Martinez glanced up the road, though Lonesome Lake was a good ten miles further along the two-lane track leading into the foothills. "Do me a favor and call me when you get back to Kenner City, so I know you made it down off the mountain safely, okay?" The sheriff rattled off a number. "Got that?"

Sophie nodded and entered the number in her sleek, sophisticated PDA, which was one of VaughnTec's newer designs. "Got it." Once she had the number keyed in, she tucked the handheld into the pocket of her stylish wool coat, keeping it close at hand.

Still, Martinez didn't look satisfied.

Getting the distinct impression that the sheriff wasn't at all happy with their plan, Griffin lowered his voice and said, "What aren't you telling us?"

Martinez grimaced, and for a moment, Griffin didn't think he was going to answer. But then the sheriff said, "Look, there have been some…incidents in this area lately. First, there was that body that turned up, the dead FBI agent?" At Griffin's nod of remembrance, he continued, "Well, after that, we found an abandoned car with a baby in it. A *baby,* for God's sake. And then one of our crime scene analysts was attacked the other day not far from here, further on toward Lonesome Lake. The weather's been playing hell with our ability to process the scenes, which is logjamming the investigations…and to top it all off, the Feds think there's a chance that Vincent Del Gardo might still be in the area." The sheriff shook his head. "Logically, those incidents probably aren't all connected, but… Just be careful up there, okay?"

Griffin muttered a curse under his breath, but nodded. "Will do."

"Call me if you need anything." The sheriff stepped back and waved them on their way, but his eyes remained dark as he watched them pass.

His figure had barely begun to recede in the distance before Sophie said, "Who is Vincent Del Gardo?"

Griffin knew he probably should have told her about the recent problems near Lonesome Lake, but to be honest, he'd all but forgotten about them. Between the HiTek negotiations, Kathleen's retirement and various other business matters he'd been juggling against his responsibility as Luke's father and his desire to be involved in as many pieces of his son's life as he possibly could be, he simply hadn't given much thought to the issues in Kenner County. He'd assumed the matter would be settled by the time the estate was completely renovated and he brought Luke and Darryn out for a visit. So he hadn't bothered updating Sophie on the situation.

Besides, it wasn't like he'd planned to bring her out to Lonesome Lake. Between the stalled negotiations, the air traffic delays and the continued problems up at the estate, it'd just been the most practical solution under the circumstances.

More or less, he thought, glancing at the ominous sky

overhead and considering just how much of his decision to drive out had been motivated by practicality, and how much had been the bloody-minded stubbornness Kathleen had accused him of more than once. He could feel the storm gathering, and a piece of him wondered if they might not be better off turning around and heading back down to the city without doing a walk-through of the lake house. But he was bound and determined to get *something* done today, and besides, the best Doppler money could buy said they had a few hours' leeway.

So instead of calling it off, he answered her question, saying, "Vincent Del Gardo is—or *was*—head of the Del Gardo crime family in Las Vegas." Griffin recalled what Martinez had told him a few weeks earlier, when the sheriff had called to ask for permission for the county's newly assembled crime scene unit, the Kenner County CSU, to search the estate and surrounding property. "About three years ago, Del Gardo was put on trial for ordering a hit on Nicky Wayne, head of the rival Wayne crime family. Del Gardo was convicted, but he escaped from the courthouse jail and disappeared. A few months ago, the body of Special Agent Julie Grainger, who'd been working the Del Gardo case, was found on a Ute reservation near here. Since then, Sheriff Martinez's people, the KCCU, the Feds and the reservation police have been investigating the murder. About a month ago, they figured out that Del Gardo used to own Lonesome Lake, and came to suspect that he might've been hiding out in the area."

"You bought your getaway from the Mob?" Sophie

asked. She had a faint wrinkle between her eyebrows, which he'd learned signaled that she'd just made a mistake, or thought he had. He'd actually learned to pay attention to the tiny frown, because when she wasn't dumping coffee on him, she had pretty good instincts.

"No way." He shook his head in adamant denial. "Del Gardo owned the property through a shell company. It was well-hidden, and not something that even the best due diligence would've turned up. The Del Gardo family went into a financial skid after Vincent disappeared, so they liquidated a bunch of assets, including Lonesome Lake. My purchasing the place was totally on the up-and-up. Once the Feds figured out the connection between Del Gardo and Lonesome Lake, though, and given that Agent Grainger's body was found in Kenner County, they wanted the KCCU to go through the house, just to be sure Del Gardo wasn't hiding there. They searched the mansion backward and forward and didn't find anything. I think they even did a few flyovers of the mountainside, looking for infrared signatures and such. Nothing. Del Gardo is long gone."

Sophie pursed her lips. "Sheriff Martinez seems to think otherwise."

Griffin glanced over at her, but beyond her faint frown, he couldn't read her mood from her face. He'd noticed before that for a young woman who by her own admission hadn't seen much of the world, she had an unusual ability to hide her feelings.

"The place is clean, but if you're worried about Del Gardo, you can stay in the car while I look around," he offered. "I just want to see what's finished and what's not, and check whether the problems that Perry has been reporting are actually as bad as he says, or if there's something else going on up at the estate. It shouldn't take more than an hour, and then we'll head back into Kenner City."

But she shook her head. "You wanted me to come along to take notes and pictures, and that's what I'm going to do. It's my job." She said the last with a hint of defiance.

Griffin nodded and slowed as the road curved and a set of pillars came into view, flanking a crushed stone driveway. "Here we are." He turned the SUV between the pillars and followed the gravel drive, which quickly gave way to the lake-spanning bridge. He eased up on the gas and let the rental roll to a stop at the edge of the bridge. "Welcome to Lonesome Lake."

Even in the gray light of the approaching storm, it was just as gorgeous as he remembered from the one time he'd visited prior to buying the property. On that day, several months earlier, the lake had been clear and blue beneath a perfect sky. Now, it was a flat expanse of white, wearing a dusting of snow over the frozen surface. The bridge, which arrowed straight across a narrow point of the lake, was a wide expanse of brick-inset concrete, with knee-high brushed-steel railings on either side to prevent cars from swerving into the water. On the far shore of the lake, the driveway went back to crushed stone and continued up through the tree line, where the lowlands merged with the foothills of the Rocky Mountains.

Partway up, rising above the level of the trees surrounding it, the large estate house looked as though it was built into the side of the mountain itself. The structure, which followed the angle of the earth beneath it, was a blend of rustic logs and modern glass. It ascended the mountain, level by level, and was topped with a partially finished solar-paneled roof. When the roof was completed, the solar panels would catch the sun and help power the massive home. For now, the estate relied on two huge diesel generators, which ran everything except the propane stoves and the well water and filtration system, which used battery-powered pumps. Off to the left of the main house, the roofs of the detached guesthouse and large barn were just visible, as well. Several smaller structure, including the lean-to that housed the generators, as well as a woodshed where the firewood was kept, were below the level of the trees, hidden among the pines.

Griffin was proud that he was able to offer his son such a cool getaway, and a place where they could be just a family, away from the pressures and posturing of San Fran society. He glanced at Sophie. "What do you think?"

"It's lovely," she breathed.

"Yeah," he agreed, the view reminding him why he'd bought Lonesome Lake rather than one of the other half dozen places he'd considered. He'd liked the isolation, yes, and he'd been able to picture himself fishing in the lake with Luke, year after year. But he'd also been drawn to the wildness of the location, the grandeur of the views and the sheer presence of the architecture.

It was a hell of a place, that was for sure.

Suddenly anxious to get inside the buildings and take a look around at what had—or hadn't—been done, he hit the gas and sent the SUV thundering across the bridge.

They were halfway across when he heard a banging noise, as though the SUV had backfired.

Moments later, the concrete surface ahead of them cracked, then sagged. Adrenaline jolted through Griffin as the SUV dropped a few inches, tilting. The damned bridge was giving way!

"Hang on!" he shouted as he hit the gas hard, flooring it. The SUV's tires screeched and the vehicle lunged forward, but it was too late. They were already sinking. Falling.

Sophie screamed as the steel railing gave way with a screech and groan. The nose of the SUV yawed downward. Griffin locked up the brakes, but that didn't help. Nothing did.

The vehicle slid ten or fifteen feet, then dropped straight down and smashed into the frozen surface of Lonesome Lake.

The crash noise roared inside the vehicle, counterpointed by Sophie's choked-off scream. Ice chunks flew up on either side of them and the airbags detonated with a *whumpf,* cushioning the force of the impact, but also pinning Griffin back against the driver's seat as the SUV nosed beneath the lake surface. Cursing, he fought the springy airbag, fought his seat belt, trying to get free.

The spiderwebbed windshield crumbled inward under the water pressure and frigid water poured in over the dashboard, dousing him. Freezing him. A clock started up in his head, timing how long they'd been in the water, and how long they could stay there, which wasn't long at all.

The SUV paused for a moment, hung up on a chunk of pylon, then slewed to the side and started to sink once again.

Griffin didn't know how deep the lake was at that location, didn't want to wait around and find out. They had to get out of the vehicle, had to reach the mansion and get themselves dried off and warm, or else hypothermia would set in quickly. He didn't know why or how the bridge had given way just as they were crossing it—maybe the passage of the construction trucks had weakened it, or the last freeze-thaw cycle had done irreparable damage. But that didn't matter just then. What mattered was getting him and Sophie to safety.

Knowing they'd gone from a business drive to a life-or-death situation in an instant, Griffin shoved his business persona aside and drew on the man he'd once been, the soldier who'd saved lives, and taken them. Fighting past the airbag, he kicked the windshield all the way out, letting in a new gush of water but clearing the way for escape. "Come on," he said. "We can—" He broke off, cursing bitterly as he got a good look at Sophie.

She was out cold. And the water was rising fast.

ON THE OTHER SIDE of the lake, the bald man leaned up against a tree and watched the SUV sink into the frozen lake.

He would've liked a cigarette to congratulate himself for a job well done, but his wife had nagged him to quit a few years back. So instead, he stood there and watched as the ice-laden water rose up around the heavily tinted rear windows of the four-by-four.

He couldn't see in through the tint, but there was no sign of the vehicle's occupants trying to escape. If Vaughn and his secretary were in a position to get out, there would've been doors flying open, and occupants scrambling out to safety. Which meant they were already dead, or close enough to it that the distinction was academic.

It was for the best, really, he thought, feeling no grief or guilt for the dead, but rather the sense of another box checked off on his to-do list. He didn't have anything against Vaughn and the woman. They had simply been in the way of more important things.

Satisfied, the man pantomimed flicking an imaginary cigarette butt to the ground and pretended to grind it into the frozen soil. Then he settled his loaded knapsack more comfortably on his back and turned away, headed back uphill toward the barn at the rear of the house.

He had a job to do. It was as simple as that. And anyone who got in his way was going to become a statistic, real quick.

Chapter Two

Sophie awoke to panic and pain. The panic was locked in her chest, squeezing her lungs and keeping the screams inside. The pain was in her head, making her dizzy and weak. And she was freezing—not just a little "time to go put on a sweater" chill—but a deep, bone-hurting cold that surrounded her, consumed her.

She struggled against the sensations, trying and failing to push away from whatever terrible nightmare gripped her. Then the world shifted, reeling around her. Light intruded, forcing her to squint against the stabbing glare.

"That's it, Sophie. In and out," a deep, masculine voice said from very close by. "You can do it. Breathe in and out."

The pressure on her lungs let up, and some of the pain cleared. The world stopped spinning and she could move again. Moments later she could see again, though seeing didn't do much to clear her confusion, because she found herself lying on her back, with her handsome boss, Griffin Vaughn, leaning over her.

In his late thirties, with short dark hair that was frosted

with silver at the temples, Griffin was a hard, no-nonsense businessman with chiseled features and elegantly arched brows. He was clipped and to the point, and rarely let his face show the slightest hint of emotion. Which was why it was shocking to see worry in his dark green eyes, and hear it in his voice when he said, "Hey. Welcome back to the land of the living. You scared the heck out of me."

"Sorry," she said inanely, too aware that his face was close enough that if she reached up just a little, they'd be kissing. Which was the sort of thought she usually relegated to the "don't go there" section of her brain, along with thoughts of her mother's illness and her own crippling debt load.

She stared up at him, blinking, trying to figure out what had happened. As she did so, she realized she wasn't really even that cold anymore, just numb, almost going to warm now, kindling to heat. She smiled, dazed. Griffin didn't smile back, though. Instead, he touched her cheek, though she barely felt it. "You're freezing."

"Not really. I'm actually sort of warm." Her voice sounded strange, a deep rasp she wasn't used to, and her throat hurt with the effort.

His expression went hard. "That's even worse, because it means you're going into hypothermia. We've got to get moving. Come on. Your arms and legs are working fine—nothing's broken. I could carry you, but I think it'd be better if you walked and got your blood moving." He eased away from her and stood, then reached down to pull her up. The world tilted beneath her feet and she sagged against him, feeling his hard, masculine muscles beneath his sopping-wet button-down shirt.

Wait a minute. Why was he wet?

Her fuzzy brain finally sharpened and she became suddenly cognizant of the fact that he wasn't the only one who was wet to the skin. Her own clothes were glued to her body, cold and soaking. And it was freezing out; a sharp wind cut through the pitiful protection of her wet clothing, and as she watched, a few fat flakes of snow drifted down from the leaden sky above. *The blizzard*, she thought, heart kicking with belated panic. *The bridge!*

She gasped as she remembered the accident, the pop of the airbags, and then—

What then?

Heart hammering, she pulled away from her boss and looked at the lake. The bridge was a wreck, with a big section missing from the middle and chunks of cement hanging from mangled steel reinforcements. There was no sign of the SUV.

"Wha-t-t-t…" The last word turned into a stutter when huge shivers started racking her. With the exertion of standing and beginning to move around, the numbness she'd been feeling had changed to a huge, awful coldness. Wrapping her arms around her body as her muscles locked on the chills, she turned to Griffin. "You pulled me out-t-t?"

"Come on." He slid an arm around her and urged her uphill. "We've got to get up to the house."

He was shivering, too, she realized. She could feel the tremors racking his large, masculine frame, could hear them in his voice, warning her that the two of them were far from out of danger. They could very well freeze before they reached safety.

As if called by the thought, a storm gust whistled across the lake and slammed into them, nearly driving them to the ground. Wind-driven snow peppered them, the icy pellets stinging Sophie's hands and face. The pain was a sharp heat against the background of bone-aching cold.

"It's not supposed to s-start snowing until l-later," she stuttered, not even able to feel her lips moving.

He didn't answer, just started walking, keeping a strong grip on her waist and urging her onward. Knowing he was right, they had to get moving, she put one foot in front of the other, forcing herself to keep up with his long-legged strides.

From the feel of gravel beneath her low-heeled boots—which were *not* designed for snow trekking—she figured they were following the driveway. She couldn't see it, though; it was covered with a layer of white. Snow had already blanketed the ground and frosted the trees, and more of the cold, wet stuff was plummeting down from the sky every second. Sometimes it drifted along, white and fluffy, looking almost pretty. For the most part, though, it blew sideways with stinging impact, eventually forcing her to slit her eyes against the storm. She put her head down and tried to shut out the cold and the snow, tried not to focus on anything but trudging along.

You're still on probation for this job, whether he's admitting it or not, she told herself. *Now is not the time to wimp out.*

Granted, she could argue some seriously extenuating circumstances, and even a terrifyingly in-control man such as Griffin would have to give her a pass on losing it just now. But thinking about it that way, like it was a test she needed to pass, gave her the strength to keep pushing forward.

She needed this job more than he had any reason to understand. She knew he thought she was too young and inexperienced to fill Kathleen's size-ten shoes, but she was bound and determined to do just that, because if she lost this job…

No, she wouldn't think about that, either. She'd just keep walking, keep proving herself.

They struggled against the wind, headed toward the mountainside house, which had seemed very close when they'd been driving over the bridge, but now felt very far away. Eventually they passed into the tree line and the wind abated slightly, but the steady incline of the driveway sapped Sophie's strength, and the temperature was dropping with the incoming storm. She'd all but stopped shivering, which she knew was a bad sign, and a glance at Griffin showed that his face reflected the gray of the sky, and his lips were tinged with blue.

They didn't have much time left.

He caught her look, met her eyes, and in his expression she saw only determination, and a flat-out refusal to admit defeat. Sounding far more like a drill sergeant than the efficient businessman she'd come to know over the past month, he growled, "Move your ass. That's an order."

If he'd coddled, she might have given in. Instead, the grating rasp of his voice had her stiffening her spine, gritting her teeth and forging onward as the snowfall thickened, going from stinging ice to fat flakes that whipped around them, swirling and turning the world to white. They were no longer a mismatched pair of boss and assistant—they were just two very cold human beings struggling to reach the basics: shelter and warmth. Safety.

Sophie's breath burned in her lungs, and her muscles felt dead and leaden. She stumbled and caught herself, stumbled again and would've fallen if it hadn't been for Griffin looping a strong arm around her waist. His silent strength urged her to keep going, not to give up.

Then, miraculously, the snow-covered surface beneath their feet changed, going from gravel to rough-edged cement bricks. Sophie jerked her head up and peered through her ice-encrusted lashes, and gave a cry of joy when she saw that they'd reached a parking area that encircled a central planting bed. Beyond that was the modern, pillar-fronted house.

"Come on, we're almost there!" Griffin said, shouting encouragement over the howling wind.

Through the whipping ice pellets, she could see the details that distance had obscured: the touches of stained glass on either side of the carved main doorway, and the intricate stonework and terraced landscaping leading up the walk. There were no lights, no sign of habitation, but that didn't matter. What mattered was the promise of getting out of the wind and—please, God—getting warm and dry.

The possibility spurred her on, and she felt a renewed burst of energy from Griffin, too. Together, they hurried up the wide stone steps leading to the front door. She grabbed the knob and twisted, her fingers slipping in the icy wetness. Her breath hissed between her teeth. "It's locked. D-do you have a key?"

"It's in the lake with the rest of our stuff." He cast around, kicking at several half-buried rocks that were frozen into the planting beds on either side of the entryway. When one came loose, he grabbed it, returned to where Sophie was waiting and used the rock to smash one of the narrow stained glass panels. The glass held against the first two blows, then gave way on the third, shattering inward in an act of destruction that would've bothered Sophie under any other circumstance, but in this case seemed very much like Griffin himself—direct and to the point.

He took a moment to clear the sharpest shards away from the edges, then stuck his arm through, and felt around.

"No alarms?" Sophie asked.

"Not yet," he replied, face set in concentration. "Too many workmen to bother. Besides, the cops are, what? Half an hour away? Forty minutes? Not worth it."

The reminder of how isolated they were, even more so with the incoming storm, brought a renewed chill chasing through Sophie. If Griffin hadn't gotten them safely out of the SUV, it might've been days, maybe longer before rescue personnel arrived. By then it would've been far too late.

Then again, if they didn't get warm soon, the same logic could very well apply.

The click of a deadbolt followed by the snick of a door lock came through the panel. Sophie twisted the knob, and nearly fell through when the door swung open beneath her weight. Griffin grabbed her and they piled through the door together. He kicked the panel shut at their backs, closing out most of the storm. The air went still, save for the draft that whistled through the broken window.

But it wasn't the sudden quiet that had Griffin cursing under his breath. It was the sight that confronted them, laying waste to any hope of an easy fix to their predicament.

"Oh," Sophie breathed, because there didn't seem to be much else to say.

The place was a wreck.

They were standing in a grand entryway—or what might've been a grand entryway in a previous life. Just then, though, it was bare studs and two-by-four construction, with electrical wiring spewed haphazardly around and the flooring pulled back to the plywood subfloor. The skeleton of a stairwell rose up to the right, leading to a second floor that wasn't much more than framework, and Sophie could see straight through to the back of the house, where nailed-down tarps seemed to be substituting for the back wall.

Worse, it wasn't much warmer inside than out, and she didn't hold much hope for a working heat source if the rest of the place looked as rough as the entryway. No doubt the hot water heater was off-line. Probably the electricity, too.

"Son of a bitch." Griffin took two steps away from her and stood vibrating with fury, his hands balled into fists. "That thieving bastard. Look what he's done to this place. That no-good, lying—" He snapped his teeth shut on the building tirade, and shook his head. "Never mind. I'll kill him later."

Sophie was startled by the threat, and by how natural it sounded, as though her slick businessman boss might actually be capable of hurting his contractor. Then again, she realized, looking at him now, this wasn't the Griffin Vaughn she'd grown more or less used to over the past month. He was wet, cold and angry, and should've looked like an absolute mess in wringing wet business clothes furred with globs of melting snow. But he didn't. He looked capable and masculine, and somehow larger than before.

He glanced over at her, his eyes dark, but softening a hint when he looked at her. "Let's get moving. There's got to be at least one room that still has walls and a working fireplace. That may be the best we can hope for."

Sophie nodded shakily. Trying to force her rapidly fuzzing brain to work, she said, "The housekeeper and her husband live here, right?"

He snapped his fingers. "Good call. Gemma and Erik are gone, but they've been doing the repairs to their quarters personally. Erik didn't want anyone else messing with his space. Which means there's a good chance that their apartment is in better shape than this disaster area. It's probably even still got electricity." He gestured off to the left, where drywall had been hung in a few places, though not taped or mudded. "Their quarters are in the back corner."

She expected him to head off and leave her to follow, reverting to business as usual now that they were, at the very least, out of the whipping wind. Instead, he took her arm, which probably meant she looked as bad as she felt. Telling herself she could be tough and self-reliant once they found someplace to hunker down and get warm, Sophie leaned into him as they walked down a short hallway, skirting drop cloths and torn-up sections of flooring.

"Obviously the generator's not running, but it's a standard model. I should be able to get it going again," Griffin said, sounding as though he was thinking aloud. "If not, hopefully Gemma and Erik's fireplace will be usable. I'd say we should try the guesthouse if we don't have any luck here, but Perry stripped it last month after the pipes froze and burst, and the barn and woodshed have zero in the way of amenities." He shot her a wry look. "If worse comes to worst, we can lay out some kitchen tile and build a campfire on it. There's plenty of scrap wood."

"True enough," Sophie murmured.

Moments later, they reached a closed door. Griffin tried the knob. "Locked." He glanced at her. "In this case, expediency trumps privacy."

Putting his shoulder to the door, he braced against it, half turned the knob and then gave a sort of combined jerk-kick that looked as if he'd practiced it to perfection. The door popped open, swinging inward to reveal a simply furnished sitting room.

"Thank God," Sophie breathed. Telling herself not to wonder where he'd learned how to pop a door off its lock without breaking any of the surrounding wood, she stumbled through the door.

Gemma and Erik's apartment proved to be a small, simply furnished suite done mostly in neutral beiges and browns, with accents of rust and navy. There was a kitchen and bathroom off to one side of the sitting room, and two doors leading from the other side. Sophie made a beeline for the doors. One opened into a small office filled with landscaping books and magazines. The other yielded pay dirt, not in the neat queen-size bed and southwestern-print curtains, but in the dresser and his-and-hers closets, which were full of clothes.

Wonderful, warm, dry clothes.

There were also photographs everywhere, scattered around the room in a variety of wood and metal frames. Even though she was freezing, Sophie couldn't help pausing for a quick scan of the pictures. She'd always been fascinated by families, and that was clearly what these photographs chronicled: a man and woman's lifetime together.

The earliest of the pictures showed the couple mugging for the camera from atop a pair of bored-looking horses in Western tack, against a backdrop of purplish mountains and a wide-open sky. The woman looked to be in her early twenties, dark-haired and pretty, with regular features and an open, engaging smile. Her eyes twinkled with mischief. The man was maybe a few years older, blond and fair-skinned, with the beginnings of a sunburn. He was looking at her with an expression of complete and utter adoration.

The other photos showed the couple at different points in their lives together—their wedding; a baby, then two; family candids as the children grew. The man's hair went from blond to white, while the woman's stayed relentlessly—and perhaps unnaturally—dark brown, but her face softened with age, and living. There were other weddings, other vacations, until the last photo, which sat on the beside table and showed just the man and the woman, in their late fifties, maybe early sixties, wrapped around each other at the edge of Lonesome Lake, with the now-demolished bridge in the background.

The woman's expression still twinkled with mischief. The man still had eyes only for her. That love, and the sense of family unity that practically jumped out of the photos, put an uncomfortable kink in Sophie's windpipe, right in the region of her heart.

"Here." Griffin appeared in the doorway behind her and tossed an armload of terrycloth towels on the bed, having apparently raided the bathroom. He moved past her and rooted through the dresser and closet, coming up with jeans, a shirt and thick sweater, along with two pairs of wool socks and a worn men's belt. Then he headed back out, saying over his shoulder, "You take this room, I'll change in the office." Then he paused in the doorway. "What's wrong?"

"Nothing." She made herself move away from the bedside photo and start picking through the dresser. "I'm guessing we're out of luck in the shower department?"

"Sorry. The pump is battery-powered, so we've got running water, but it's going to be cold. I'll have to get the generator going for hot water. First, though, I want to get us dry and see about starting a fire."

Sophie nodded. "Of course." As he left the room, she pawed through the dresser, telling herself not to waste time feeling squeamish about going through a stranger's things. The worst of the bone-numbing cold had eased now that they were out of the storm, but getting dry and warm was still a major priority.

"I'll reimburse them for the clothes," Griffin said unexpectedly from the other room. "So stop stalling. If I don't hear you getting naked in the count of ten, I'm coming in and doing it for you."

From another man the words might've been a tease, or a threat. Coming from laconic Griffin Vaughn, who didn't seem to suffer from the same zing of chemistry Sophie felt every time she was within five feet of him, they were simply a fact. As far as she could tell, he hadn't even noticed she was female—theirs was purely a business relationship. Or rather, the possibility of one, if she worked very hard and managed not to dump any more coffee on him.

Unfortunately, she got clumsy when she was nervous, and something about the way he looked in the throes of negotiation—all stern-faced and dark-eyed, with a flash of excitement when he moved in for the coup de grâce—well, that made her all too aware that he was male. Which made her nervous, and therefore clumsy.

"Sophie?" Griffin called, and his low-voiced inquiry buzzed along her nerve endings like liquid fire, the heat brought by the thought of him undressing her, and focusing all that dark-eyed intensity on her.

But the threat got her moving, and she started stripping out of her wet, clinging clothes. "You don't have to come in," she called after a moment. "I'm naked." She blushed at the echo of her own words, bringing stinging warmth to her cheeks. "Never mind. Forget I said that, okay?"

She grabbed the towels he'd left for her and scrubbed them over her skin, warming some life back into her chilled flesh, which seemed strange and disconnected, as though it didn't belong to her anymore. Soon, though, life began to return—pins and needles at first, then stinging pain. Skin that had been fish-belly-white moments earlier flared to angry red, and she hissed with the return of feeling as she drew on a pair of borrowed jeans and a turtleneck, socks and thick sweater.

She soon realized that she and Gemma were built very differently: the other woman was taller and significantly narrower in the hips and bust. Doing the best with what she had, Sophie rolled up the cuffs to deal with the too-long jeans, and hoped the sweater was loose enough to disguise how tightly the clothes fit across her chest and rear. Like Griffin, she skipped borrowing underwear, instead going commando beneath her clothing.

Logic said that shouldn't have felt daring under the circumstances, but she was acutely aware of the chafe of material against her unprotected skin as she left the bedroom. Not that he would notice, because he was all about business. Which was a relief, despite the fact that she'd developed a mild crush on him. Indeed, she only allowed herself the crush *because* he wasn't interested. After what had happened at her last job, where she'd been romanced and played by a jerk of the first degree, and said jerk had set out to destroy her career options, the last thing Sophie was looking to do was get romantically involved with her boss. No thanks, not going there again.

Heading out of the bedroom into the main sitting area, Sophie found Griffin crouched by the fireplace. Kindling and mid-sized logs were neatly organized in a burnished copper tub to one side of the hearth, and a small drift of ashes and charred wood inside the fireplace suggested it was fully functional, which was very good news indeed.

Griffin had used some of the kindling to build a neat teepee, with crumpled paper in the center, and a trio of larger logs crossed in a tripod arching over the kindling. The setup, like the hip-check he'd used to open the door, looked practiced and professional, which didn't fit with the image of the polished businessman she'd spent the past month assisting.

The Griffin Vaughn she worked for wore custom

suits and monogrammed shirts, yet cared little for fashion. His entire focus was centered on VaughnTec. He was seeking to grow the company by shrinking their products even further while increasing the functionality of each unit. VaughnTec, which was part R & D, part mass market, combined cameras, computers, phones, music, video games and a host of other functionalities into small handheld units so simple that even the technologically challenged could figure them out within a few minutes. It was Griffin who'd moved the company in that direction when he'd taken it over from his uncle, Griffin who'd made it into the powerhouse it was today. He was ruthless without being cruel, cold without being unfriendly. But even when he was being his most cordial, she'd noticed, he maintained a thick barrier between him and the world, a reserve that she'd only seen soften when he was talking to his young son, Luke, on the phone.

Despite the pressures of Sophie's job situation—i.e. that losing it was a real threat yet absolutely not an option—she had grown, if not comfortable with Griffin's business persona, at least confident that she knew where she stood with him. He was polite but not terribly friendly, and had made it obvious that he considered her too young and green for the position. But at the same time, he'd been clear about his needs and wishes, and had given her ample room to perform the tasks Kathleen had laid out for her, which had mostly consisted of scheduling his travel and juggling calls, retrieving information and hunting up the occasional meal. All of those things were well within the skills she'd learned in the courses she'd taken for certification, and if she'd fumbled a few times when nerves had overcome training, he'd seemed to let those instances go. All in all, she'd found him a tough but fair employer. Yes, he was far too attractive for her peace of mind, but she thought she understood the Griffin Vaughn she'd been working for.

However, she didn't know the Griffin Vaughn who was crouched down in front of the fireplace wearing a fisherman's sweater and faded jeans, blowing a small ember into a flame, then feeding it strips of kindling until the fire flared up and lit the teepee he'd built so carefully. Logic and what she knew about her boss suggested that he should've looked like a man completely out of his natural element. Instead, he wore the borrowed clothes like they were old familiar friends, and he moved with neat economy as he built the fire up, coaxing it to accept the first of the logs. His towel-dried hair was engagingly rumpled, making him seem younger, though his face still gave away little of the man within.

Illumination from the flames danced across his forbidding features. The warm light was a welcome contrast to the dimness outside, where the world had gone to grayish-white and the day was fading hours earlier than it should have.

The fire drew Sophie forward, even as nerves warned her not to get too close to this new version of Griffin Vaughn. She stood beside him and stretched her hands out toward the fire, but felt little relief from the cold.

"It'll need to warm the brickwork before much heat starts bouncing out into the room," Griffin said.

"Were you an Eagle Scout or something?" she asked, unable to help herself, because too many things weren't quite lining up between this Griffin and the one she thought she knew.

"Or something." He rose, dusting the ash from his hands, and wound up standing very near her. Too near.

She could see the hints of hazel in his green eyes, saw them darken when tension snapped into the air between them. She was suddenly very aware of his height and strength, and the way the smell of wood smoke fit with the sight of him in jeans and a sweater—raw, masculine and elemental. And in that instant, she realized she'd been wrong about at least one thing: Griffin most definitely knew she was a woman. The knowledge was in his eyes, which were more alive than she'd ever seen them.

Heat flared suddenly, not from the fireplace, but within her. The warmth spread from her core to her extremities, which still tingled with the aftereffects of the freezing conditions, and the danger they'd survived together.

Maybe it was that danger that had her leaning into him, maybe it was the attraction she'd told herself to ignore all these weeks. Either way, she was suddenly very close to him, and he to her, their lips a breath apart.

A log shifted in the fireplace, sending sparks. The noise startled her, breaking through the sensual fog and slapping her with a shout from her subconscious. *Danger!*

Grabbing hold of herself, she took a big step back, away from the fireplace. Away from the man. As she did so, she was aware that he did the exact same thing, levering himself away. In that moment, she saw the shields drop back down over his expression, distancing him more surely than the floor space now separating them. Suddenly, he was no longer a regular guy starting a fire in the fireplace; he was a millionaire businessman who ate small companies for breakfast, and just happened to be wearing a sweater and jeans.

More important, he was her boss.

Heat rushed to Sophie's cheeks and she berated herself for being stupid, for getting too close to the line with the man who had far too much control over her future, more than he even realized. "I'm sorry," she whispered. "I shouldn't have—"

"I'm going out," he interrupted, heading for the door, where he grabbed a pair of tired-looking boots and a heavy, bright-red waterproof parka, borrowing more of Erik's clothing. "I want to look around a little and get the generators going. There are a bunch of outbuildings—barns, a guesthouse, that sort of thing. I want to make sure they're as secure as they're going to get before the main force of the storm hits. I'd appreciate it if you'd check the kitchen and see about some food. Do you still have your PDA in your coat?"

A unit of his own design, the PDAs combined a phone, computer and GPS functionalities into a single small unit.

Sophie nodded. "Yes, I do. But won't it have shorted out?" They were seriously useful little machines, but still, they were machines.

"Sometimes the little buggers come back to life after they've gotten wet. Say, for instance, after a toddler tries to flush one of them." His expression softened a hair at the tangential mention of his son, but his eyes stayed cool on hers, as though he was waiting to see what she would do next, how she would handle herself in the aftermath of the sensually charged moment they'd just shared.

She was going to ignore it, that was what she was going to do, Sophie decided on the spot. Just as he'd done.

Plastering a neutral expression on her face, she tried to drop herself back into the executive assistant's role, even though it didn't seem to fit quite right under the circumstances. She nodded. "Food and PDA. Got it. If I get the phone up and running, do you want me to call Sheriff Martinez and let him know what happened?"

Griffin glanced through a window, at the whiteout conditions outside. "Definitely. See if he can get someone out here to pick us up." He lifted a shoulder. "It's a long shot, but you never know. Maybe this is just a squall before the blizzard."

A howl of wind hit the side of the mansion and rattled the windows in their frames, seeming to mock the idea. Somewhere else in the house there was a crashing noise, suggesting that Perry and his work crew hadn't secured the construction zone sufficiently against the force of the incoming blizzard.

Griffin winced, but didn't say anything, just jerked on the borrowed boots, shrugged into the coat and headed for the door.

He paused at the threshold and looked back at her. "I want you to lock the deadbolt after me, and keep it locked."

He was gone before she could ask why that would be necessary, given that they were alone in the mansion. She flipped the bolt as ordered, but couldn't help wondering who he was trying to guard her from. Himself? That didn't make any sense.

She heard his footsteps recede, heard a distant door slam. Moments later, she caught a flash of his red parka as he headed, not around the generator shed, but rather straight across the parking circle and down the driveway.

He was going to look at the crash site, she realized, and the realization brought a shiver of fear as she clicked onto the one question she hadn't yet asked herself about the situation—not how they were going to manage to wait out the storm, or what would happen if she and Griffin ended up face-to-face again and they weren't smart enough to step away, but rather the all-important question they hadn't had the time to ask before. Why had the bridge given out beneath them? Was it just bad luck?

Or had it been something more sinister?

Chapter Three

The wind was sharp as hell and Griffin's core temp wasn't all the way back to normal, but he kept moving down the driveway, his booted feet sliding in the rapidly deepening snow. The visibility wasn't great, but he was certain he could make it down to the crash site and back up to the mansion before the conditions became impossible. Besides, the longer he waited, the less likely he was to find anything useful.

If, of course, there was anything to find.

Maybe it was just a flat-out coincidence that he and Sophie had been in the SUV that broke the camel's back, so to speak. Maybe it was simply that their vehicle had finally overloaded the time-stressed cement bridge and brought it crashing down.

Thing was, he wasn't a big believer in coincidence. That lesson had been hard learned in the service, and his years in the business world had only reinforced his conviction that everything happened for a reason, and that anything could be prevented from happening twice if he was smart enough, disciplined enough. Controlled enough.

At the thought of control, he flashed back to what had just happened in front of the fireplace, when he'd almost lost the self-discipline he prided himself on. He'd very nearly given in to temptation and kissed Sophie. What was more, she would've welcomed his kiss; he'd seen it in her eyes, felt it in the tension-laden air.

The attraction was there, had been there from the first moment she'd walked into his office. He'd managed to tamp it down to an awareness, and she'd hidden the fact, as well. Most of the time, anyway. But that moment in front of the fireplace had shattered their pretense of disinterest. And damned if that wasn't going to complicate things, big time, not just over the next couple of days if they wound up snowed in together, but over the longer term, as well. He couldn't afford to get tangled up with another woman who wanted to trade affection for a step up in life.

It wasn't that he thought Sophie was playing him, either. His instincts said she was exactly what she seemed: a young, relatively inexperienced woman who was getting a late start in the workforce for whatever reason, and was earnest in her efforts to do a good job. But that didn't mean she wouldn't set her sights higher if he gave her reason to think it was a possibility.

That wasn't ego talking, either. It was just the way he'd learned the world worked. And if that felt faintly disloyal to the memory of his own childhood, it couldn't be helped. His parents had met and fallen in love in a very different time, and they'd been lucky to find a perfect match in each other. He'd tried to find the same sort of match and failed. Worse, the last failure had hurt his son, as well. There was no way he was putting Luke—or himself—through another such ordeal.

They were fine on their own. There was nothing wrong with it being just the guys. In fact, the only thing wrong with the arrangement was the extensive traveling Griffin had to do for work, while Luke stayed behind in San Fran with Darryn. Then again, it was a huge relief knowing Luke was safe at home, especially given that Griffin didn't yet know exactly what sort of a situation he was dealing with.

His musings had occupied him on the half-mile trek down to the bridge. Now, as he got within sight of the wrecked span, he once again replayed those last few moments before it had given way. He remembered a banging noise, like a backfire. Or maybe an explosion. But seriously, what were the chances someone had rigged the bridge? And why?

Unfortunately, he could make an all too plausible case for the "why." When Sophie called to set up the meeting with Perry, she'd mentioned that she and Griffin were planning to tour the estate that afternoon, before the storm hit. What if the contractor was more than just shoddy or a little crooked? What if the delays were only the surface of the problem, and Perry was actually up to something even more devious, something that he couldn't afford to let an outsider see? The theory might seem pretty farfetched, but the contractor had given Griffin some seriously negative vibes the last few times they'd spoken. At the time, Griffin had assumed

Perry was spooked by his run of bad luck on the project, and rightfully fearing for his job.

Now, as Griffin worked his way out to the place where the bridge had collapsed, testing each step as he went, he wondered whether Perry had perhaps been afraid of something else entirely, like his employer finding out about dire doings up at Lonesome Lake. And if so, whether the contractor had decided to slow him down, or worse.

When Griffin reached the edge and looked down, he cursed, giving up any hope he might've had of recovering his and Sophie's suitcases or computer bags. There was no sign of the SUV, save for a rough patch where it had broken through the ice, and even that was rapidly smoothing over to snowy sameness.

"Son of a bitch," he grated, liking the situation even less than he had before. For the duration of the storm, it looked like he and Sophie were going to be down to borrowed clothes and a doused PDA.

And each other.

As TIME PASSED and Griffin still didn't return, Sophie kept herself moving because she figured it was better than working herself into a state of panic.

Deciding she'd give her boss another half hour before she went out looking for him, she turned to the tasks he'd given her: pulling together some food and rebooting her PDA. She started by making a survey of the supplies in Gemma's pantry, and quickly realized they were in pretty good shape in the nonperishable food department. The shelves were crammed with canned goods, along with glass jars of pasta sauce and home-made preserves. There was plenty of dried pasta, along with pancake mix and coffee, and even powdered eggs and milk.

"Looks like you're prepared to be snowed in for the entire winter," Sophie said to the absent housekeeper. The thought wasn't particularly cheering.

Deciding to keep it simple, in case the meal had to wait while she went out looking for Griffin, Sophie added tap water to a can of condensed tomato soup, and broke out a box of mac and cheese, knowing firsthand that it tasted fine made with powdered milk and no butter. Once she had the pasta cooking, she headed out into the main room, where a welcome sight greeted her, namely the telltale wink of an LED light from her PDA.

"Aha. A sign of life." Relieved by the thought that they might not be completely cut off from the outside world, she crossed to the unit and pressed a few buttons, shutting down the handheld computer and then power-ing it back up to see if it would come fully online.

When it did, it showed her a half charge on the battery and a weak but tenable network signal. Crossing her fingers that the call would go through, she phoned Sheriff Martinez.

He answered on the second ring. "Ms. LaRue? Are you back in the city? That was quick."

"Hi, Sheriff. And no, we're not even close to being down off the mountain." Sophie sketched out the situa-tion, trying to give the facts as calmly as she could, even though it wasn't easy to keep a tremor out of her voice as she described their plunge into Lonesome Lake and the harrowing trek up to the house.

There was a long pause after she finished, and then Martinez said, "Okay, here's the problem we're going to be facing. That snow out there? It's the real deal. The blizzard got here faster than predicted and is likely to be here for a good long time. Two days, maybe three. More importantly, the road up to Lonesome Lake goes through a pass that's impossible to keep clear during a storm. Which means you're going to be stuck there until the blizzard blows itself out."

She heard something else in his voice, and asked the same question Griffin had earlier. "What aren't you telling me?"

There was another, longer pause. "Maybe Vaughn should call me when he gets back in."

"We'll have to conserve the battery on this phone," she said, too aware that unless Griffin managed to rescue their chargers from the SUV, they were going to have to make her half-charged battery last. "So why don't you just tell me whatever it is that you'd rather tell him?" Nerves had her edging toward irritation more quickly than she would have otherwise. "I *am* a fully functional grown-up, you know."

"Yes, ma'am," the sheriff said politely, "but you're not a highly decorated marine TecSpec with some serious combat experience."

Her breath whistled between her teeth at that. "Are you saying that Griffin is?"

"Yes, ma'am. It popped up on the background check we ran as part of the Del Gardo investigation. So the way I'm figuring it, if you had to be stranded up at Lonesome Lake for a few days, you picked a pretty useful guy to be stuck with."

"I didn't pick him," she murmured automatically, but her brain was spinning.

Eagle Scout, indeed. He'd been a marine, had he? Well, that probably explained the skills he possessed that were decidedly non-MBA-approved, and the quiet reserve that sometimes seemed as much about survival as it did business. And yeah, under their current circumstances it helped her to know that he could deal with dangerous situations better than the average tycoon—if there was such a thing. But at the same time, the revelation put a serious shiver down the back of her neck.

She hadn't known about his military service. What else didn't she know about him?

A tap at the door to the apartment had her spinning with a gasp. She relaxed only slightly when Griffin's voice said, "It's me."

"What's wrong?" the sheriff asked quickly, still on the phone.

"Griffin's back." She unbolted the door and let him through, then held out the phone. "The sheriff wants to talk to you."

He nodded and shucked out of his gloves and parka, and hung them near the door, where a mat was set out to catch the wet. When he reached for the phone, his fingers brushed against Sophie's. Warmth kicked at the contact, but she forced herself not to jerk away, forced herself to act as though she hadn't felt a thing.

From the way his green eyes darkened, though, he knew. And he'd felt it, too.

So much for there being a safe distance between them. She had a feeling the next few days were going to be very dangerous to her equilibrium. But she needed this job. She needed to be able to stay in San Fran near the facility where her mother was being treated now, and she needed to make a good enough salary to cover more than the bare minimum payments on her various loans. Which meant she couldn't risk making the same mistake she'd made at her last job. What was more, she couldn't risk Griffin knowing about that mistake. Kathleen had overlooked the rumors and hired Sophie anyway, but Sophie had a feeling Griffin wouldn't be nearly so sanguine about it. The members of upper crust San Fran society tended to stick together.

After a moment, Griffin nodded, though neither of them had said anything. Then he took the phone, headed into the office and shut the door behind him.

Sophie stood for a moment, staring after him. Irritation rose. Granted, he was the boss, and he certainly had the right to take private calls in private. Hell, he'd have that right even if their roles were reversed. But what could possibly be private about a conversation with Sheriff Martinez? Whatever the sheriff was telling Griffin, it had to be related to the situation out at Lonesome Lake…and that most definitely involved her.

Setting her teeth, she marched toward the office. She

wasn't sure what she was going to do when she got there, but that didn't matter because the door opened before she reached it, and Griffin stood there, filling the doorway with his face set in harsh, unyielding lines.

She halted an arm's length away, tension coiling in her stomach. "What's wrong?"

"Perry's wife hasn't spoken to him since right after you called to tell him we were coming to meet with him." He paused, and held up his hand to show her a slender wire attached to a round, circular metal scrap, which he held pinched between his thumb and forefinger. "And I found this down by the bridge."

She stared. "What is it?" she asked, even though on some level she already knew.

"A piece from a radio-controlled detonator. The bridge didn't just give way. Somebody blew the damn thing out from underneath us."

GRIFFIN WATCHED Sophie's color drain and hoped she didn't pass out on him. If she did, though, he'd deal with it, just as he was doing his best to deal with the situation that was developing around them.

After finding the detonator scraps and evidence of a blast pattern, he'd raced back to the mansion, hoping to hell he'd find Sophie intact, that the bomber hadn't been waiting for them to split up before he made his move. But there was no sign of the bomber, no evidence of another move.

So what now? He didn't know.

His first instinct had been to not tell her about the

bomb, which was why he'd talked to the sheriff in private. That wasn't because he was trying to keep her from worrying, either. It was more that he was used to keeping the most important pieces of information to himself. Whether in battle or in business, information was power. Besides, he was used to being alone, dealing with things alone, and didn't see any need to share.

After talking to the sheriff, though, the business side of him had overtaken the soldier, and he'd reconsidered. Logic said that Sophie needed to know about the potential danger. What if the bomber was still somewhere on the estate? Given how quickly the storm had come up, that seemed like a distinct possibility. If he—and Griffin was assuming it was a he, based on general chauvinism and his gut-level belief that his contractor was the culprit—had stashed a truck on one of the rear access roads that wound through the forest surrounding the estate, he might've gotten away before the blizzard hit. But if not, there was a good chance that he'd gotten caught in the storm just as Griffin and Sophie had been…and in the same location.

So Griffin told Sophie about the bomb, showed her the detonator cap, and described the crash scene and what he'd noticed of the blast pattern, even though a piece of him wanted to shield her from the ugly truth.

As he spoke, a range of emotions crossed her face, shock and understanding, followed by a flash of anger and then outright fear.

"Somebody tried to kill us," she said softly.

"Yeah." He didn't try to sugarcoat. "Looks like it."

She was badly shaken; her light brown eyes were wide in her pale face, and she leaned a shoulder against the door frame as though that was the only thing holding her up. The chivalry his mother had worked to instill in him said that he should go to her, comfort her. Instead, he stayed put. He didn't trust the protective feelings that had kicked in the moment he realized she might be in danger, didn't like how they had threatened to overwhelm the logic that said he and Sophie were far better off keeping a professional distance.

After a moment, the shock started to fade and he could see Sophie begin to think it through. Her faint frown crinkled the skin between her eyebrows, and she said, "Did the sheriff have any idea who might've set the explosives?"

"He's reserving judgment." Actually, Martinez had cursed his head off, cursed the storm, and then cursed Griffin for being a pigheaded idiot who'd insisted on driving into the teeth of an oncoming blizzard.

Griffin couldn't argue with any of his points, either. However, what was done was done, and they could only go forward from there. Which meant figuring out who had tried to kill them, and whether he was still on the property. Either way, they needed to fortify the apartment, get it as safe as they possibly could, and then hunker down to wait out the storm.

Martinez seemed to think that the sophisticated detonator suggested the work of a professional, but Griffin disagreed. Just about anyone with a military background and a passing familiarity with explosives could've bought and used the device. That was one of the down-sides of the Internet. And surprise, surprise, when Griffin had pressed, Martinez had admitted that Perry was ex-army. The sheriff's reluctance had also warned Griffin of something else, namely that Martinez and the contractor were friendly.

Which, in his experience with smaller jurisdictions, meant that the sheriff might be less than forthcoming with important information. Indeed, the sheriff hadn't wanted to tell Sophie about the contractor's apparent disappearance, he'd waited to tell Griffin, then let him decide whether to share the info. That was probably less about Martinez being a small-town cop and more about him not wanting to frighten Sophie more than necessary, Griffin figured. He'd told her, though. She needed to know what they were up against.

Sophie's eyes narrowed as she looked at him, guess-ing something from his expression. "You think you know who it was, don't you?" She straightened away from the door frame. "Is someone after you? Is this about the HiTek acquisition?" But she shook her head, answering her own question. "No, that doesn't make sense. They're out in New York, and they wouldn't have known we were coming here. Which means it's some-one here, either someone who wants to hurt one of us—presumably you, because I'm not the sort of person who'd pop up on anyone's radar screen—or someone trying to keep people away from Lonesome Lake." Her eyes snapped to his. "Vincent Del Gardo."

Frankly, Griffin found it unnerving that her thought

process had taken her there so quickly. He'd known she was intelligent—there was no way she could've picked up the vagaries of his work and the business research he'd been asking her to do without being smart. But he never would've expected her mind to work that way. "Let's not jump to conclusions, especially when even Martinez admitted there's no evidence that Del Gardo has been anywhere in the vicinity for several months. Besides, there's another alternative. Perry Long."

The wrinkle between her eyebrows deepened. "You think your contractor tried to kill us? Why, so you wouldn't figure out that he's been billing you for repairs while gutting the house and selling off the material? Because that's sure what it looks like he's been doing."

"He'd think of the bomb as a way for him to protect himself," Griffin countered. "Especially if there's more to it than just the renovations. What if he's got something going on up here that he doesn't want anyone to know about? Something he thought he could be done with by the time I wanted to come out and see the place?"

"Such as?"

"I don't know," he admitted. "But I intend to find out. Martinez said he'd have two of his people, a Callie MacBride of the KCCU and forensic investigator Ava Wright, go back over the evidence they collected when they searched the estate, and see if they can come up with any ideas. In the meantime, we need to dig in and get ourselves prepared to wait out the storm."

Sophie nodded, pale but resolute. "Tell me what to do and I'll do it. We're in this together."

He glanced around the room. The soldier in him liked the ground-floor location, which gave them escape options. But he didn't like the idea of someone outside being able to see in, without being seen in the swirling snow. "I want you to pull all the shades and keep the lights to a minimum when it gets dark. I saw some kerosene lanterns in the office, and some candles in the bedroom."

"I found a couple of flashlights in the kitchen," Sophie volunteered.

"Good, I'll take one, you keep one. Conserve the batteries, though. We won't know about electricity until I check out the generator and the electrical panel."

"You didn't do that while you were out there?" she asked, sending him a sidelong look.

"I wanted to get back here and see about the PDA. Figured Martinez needed to know about the bridge ASAP." Griffin left out the part where he'd nearly panicked, thinking he'd left her alone in the house, wide open to attack.

He'd only responded that way because she was his responsibility. Logically, she wouldn't be in this situation if he'd listened to her and put off the trip to Lonesome Lake. Instead he'd dragged her straight into danger, albeit unwittingly. But unwitting or not, the danger was a fact, and it was up to him to make sure she didn't suffer because of his miscalculation.

"The signal's weak and I've got maybe half a charge on the battery," she said about the PDA.

"Leave it out so I can call home a little later, okay?"

"Will do. You want me to hold the food until you've restarted the generator?"

"Please. And there's another thing." Griffin headed for the bedroom and pulled out one of the drawers on Erik's side of the dresser. Just as Martinez had said it would be, there was a .45 nestled in the back, beside a box of ammo. Returning to the main room, Griffin loaded the weapon while Sophie's eyes got big. He held it out, butt first. "I want you to keep this with you while I'm gone. Just in case."

She held up her hands in a "no thanks" gesture. "You take it. I wouldn't know what to do with it."

"It's easy. This is the safety, this is the trigger." He pointed them out, then pantomimed the actions as he said, "Safety off, point the gun, pull the trigger. Boom, done."

She stared at him, expression clouding. "You think he's still up here, don't you?"

"It's a possibility," he hedged. In reality, his soldier's instincts, which he found were coming back online quickly even though he'd been a civilian for nearly seven years now, had started chiming a warning on his hike down the mountain. Finding the detonator had only confirmed what his instincts were saying: he and Sophie weren't alone.

"Then I should come with you. I can stand lookout while you work on the generator."

"You'll distract me," he said bluntly. "Cover the windows, stay near the center of the space and keep the gun with you. I'll be quick, I swear, and when I get back we'll rig a trip wire around the perimeter, so we'll have some warning if anyone tries to get at us."

It took a long moment, but finally she swallowed hard, nodded, and took the .45 from him. "Okay. Make it quick."

"I will." He suited up again in Erik's boots and parka, thinking for a moment of the man who usually wore the clothes, and how he might feel under the circumstances, having to leave behind the woman he'd been married to for nearly three decades. "Lock up behind me," Griffin said, his voice rasping on the words.

"Of course." Sophie crossed the distance between them, and though he knew she only intended to throw the deadbolt once he was gone, he had a fleeting thought that she was going to kiss him goodbye, or good luck.

That would be what a man like Erik could expect, the sort of man who had the love of a good woman, one who would kiss him goodbye and welcome him back again when he returned. And for a crazy moment, Griffin wanted to be that man. He wanted to kiss Sophie, wanted to know she'd be waiting for him, and that they'd have the long winter's night ahead of them, together in the fire-lit darkness, with the storm doing nothing more dangerous than insulating them from the outside world for a few days.

And, Griffin thought, he'd clearly hit his head when the SUV fell through the bridge. He didn't remember doing so, and didn't have a bump on his scalp, but that was the only rational explanation for the completely ir-rational urge.

There was no arguing that Sophie was a lovely wom-an. More than that, she was vivid and alive, and proving to be so much more than he'd thought upon first meeting her. She was clever and interactive, and a stronger business asset than he'd expected. And yes, she was gorgeous and single, and he was a red-blooded human male, and just about any guy would have a few "let's get closer" thoughts under the circumstances. But that was just it, he wasn't just any guy, and he had more than just his own needs to think about.

"Lock up," he repeated, pushed through the door and slammed it at his back. Though his survival instincts were shrilling for him to get out of there and do it fast, he stopped and waited, needing to hear the deadbolt click safely into place before he left.

But it didn't click. Instead, the door opened and Sophie stepped through, wearing Gemma's boots and parka, and carrying the .45.

"What in the hell do you think you're doing?" he demanded, glaring at her.

She lifted her chin and glared right back. "I'm watching your back, that's what I'm doing. You can accept it and we can move on, or I can pretend to listen when you order me back inside, and then I'll follow you from a distance. Your choice. Either way, I'm coming with you. It's stupid for me to stay behind when I could be helping."

He glared a moment longer, but saw that her mind was made up. And truthfully, she had a point. Yes, he'd be distracted if she was there, but he'd be worried about her regardless. And a lookout was never a bad thing.

"Fine." He snapped off a nod. "Don't slow me down. And for crap's sake, don't point the gun at me."

Flicking on his flashlight and keeping the beam low, he started moving down the hallway, headed for the corner of the building closest to the generator shed. He heard her footsteps and the rustle of clothing right behind him as she fell into step, bringing up the rear of their two-person army.

And damned if he didn't feel a little better, after all.

THE MOMENT THE BALD MAN slid open the door to the barn, where he'd been hiding out in a corner of the loft, he knew he'd miscalculated. Not because the snow was still whipping down from a gray-cast sky, though that would certainly slow him down, but because he smelled wood smoke.

Someone had lit a fire nearby, most likely at the main mansion, which was the only structure even halfway to livable, and at that, only in the servant's quarters. Since the staff was long gone, that could only mean one thing: he'd left the scene of the crash too quickly. Griffin Vaughn and his secretary must've somehow gotten to safety, after all. Lucky them.

Too bad for them, their luck had just run out.

Chapter Four

Sophie couldn't decide if she was proud of herself for taking a stand, or appalled at the stand she'd chosen to take. Granted, if the bomber was still in the area there was no guarantee that the apartment was any safer than elsewhere…but the walls and locked door had certainly provided the illusion of safety, if nothing else.

Instead, she was out in the main house, following practically in Griffin's footprints as he searched the mansion from bottom to top and down again, making sure they were alone in the huge, gutted structure. As they searched, he was also gathering construction detritus that he deemed useful—mostly scrap metal and rope—and piling it near the apartment for use in setting a perimeter defense, or at least an early warning system. They didn't find any evidence of there being anybody else in the house, though there was a broken upstairs window that hadn't been tarped over, making Griffin wonder aloud if it had been smashed after the workmen left the site.

Sophie tried to make as little noise as possible as she

followed him from room to room, but where he seemed
to move soundlessly, gliding across the plywood subfloor and among the scattered drop cloths, she felt like
she was making a major racket, clumping along in
Gemma's too-large boots. Griffin didn't shush her,
though. He didn't say or do anything to acknowledge
her presence, hadn't done so since they'd left the apartment. She wondered if he'd tuned her out completely,
focusing on the search. If so, she envied him the ability.

She would've liked to shut her brain down, forcing
it to focus on the task at hand—watching the doorways
as they passed, staying alert for any sign of malevolent
company. Instead, she felt as though she was fighting
to corral her thoughts when they wanted to scatter in a
dozen different directions.

Her blood hummed from her standoff with Griffin,
and with fear of the man who might be stalking them,
the man who had already tried to kill them once. She
was aware of the solid, intimidating weight of the gun
she carried with her. And she was acutely conscious of
Griffin walking an arm's length ahead of her. His long-
legged strides carried him effortlessly along, and his
shoulders were straight and square beneath the
borrowed parka, making him seem larger even than
before, as though he'd grown with the need to recall his
days as a soldier.

In some ways it made her feel better, knowing that he'd
been a marine. But at the same time it left her unsettled.
The one picture she had of her father was one of him in
uniform, square-shouldered, square-jawed and capable-

looking. Like Griffin. Over the years, she'd come to associate that picture with the family she'd wished she had, the one her mother had been unable to provide.

Focus, she told herself, and shifted her grip on the .45 as they came to a renovated exterior door that still had strips of protective adhesive on the brass hardware. Griffin glanced at her. "The generator shed is on the left. Cover me from the doorway. If anything happens…" He trailed off. "Well, just try not to shoot me, okay?"

He waited for her nod before he turned the deadbolt, put his shoulder to the door, and shoved it open.

A gust of wind nearly tore the doorknob from his grasp. The gale whipped through the opening, bringing a slash of stinging ice pellets and a deep, biting cold Sophie hadn't been prepared for. She'd thought the unheated house was frigid, but that dry cool was nothing like what she stepped into as she followed Griffin through the door and out into the storm.

The whole world was white and cold and angry, the noise and power of the storm frightening. There was snow everywhere, drifting against the side of the house and over lumps and bumps of landscaping rendered unidentifiable by a thick layer of white.

The wind slammed into Sophie, sending her reeling, but her feet stayed stuck in the shin-high snow. She nearly overbalanced, would have if Griffin hadn't grabbed her free arm, stopping her mid-fall. He leaned in, so his face was close to hers, and shouted, "Forget about staying back. The storm's stronger than I thought it would be. We'll stick together."

She nodded rather than trying to out-shout the storm. Hanging on to each other for balance, and so they wouldn't lose each other in the limited visibility, they headed for the generator shed. Each step was a huge effort, each yard gained toward their destination a small victory.

Sophie's heart was pounding and the frigid air was burning in her lungs by the time they reached the narrow exterior room that housed the generators. It was an elaborate lean-to built off the main structure, with metal sheeting she assumed was a firebreak separating it from the rest of the mansion. There were large vents at either end, no doubt intended to keep the generator fumes from building up.

Those vents also let in the cold and the blowing snow, she realized as soon as Griffin had cleared the double doors and opened the slider enough for the two of them to squeeze through. The interior was sheltered against the wind but the inside air wasn't much warmer than outside, and small drifts of white powder had collected beneath the vents.

"Not very weatherproof in here," she noted, taking a look around the narrow room, which housed two big machines, along with assorted wiring and heavy dials.

"We won't stay long," Griffin said. "Just keep watching."

"Watching what? You can't see three feet in front of yourself out there." But she took position by the open door, squinting into the too-white world of the storm.

Griffin took a circuit around the room, checking another set of doors at the far end of the lean-to, and paying close attention to one set of dials. Seeming satisfied, he turned to the nearer of the two big machines and started fiddling with the control panel. Catching Sophie's glance in his direction, he called, "There's no sign that it's been tampered with, and no sign of charges or a timer having been set. I think we're okay to start it up."

Since she hadn't been worried about the possibility of the big generators being sabotaged until just that second, she could only nod, and then close her eyes when he hit the button to start the generator.

The machine purred to life, and she let out a relieved breath. "Next time you think there's a chance something might blow up on us, warn me, okay?"

He raised an eyebrow. "Would it have helped you to know ahead of time?"

Probably not, she admitted inwardly. Aloud, she said, "Did you do this sort of thing a lot when you were in the marines?"

"Who told you about that?"

"The sheriff, on the phone." She let her earlier question hang. It was prying to ask about his time in the marines, she knew. But she wanted to hear him say that what they were going through was no big deal, that he'd survived worse. She didn't even think she would care if it was a lie, as long as she could pretend everything was going to be okay.

Seeming to understand, Griffin crossed to the doorway and stopped very near her, close enough that she could see the beginnings of a beard shadowing his jawline, and the uncompromising glint in his dark green eyes. "I was a TecSpec, which means I was the gadget guy, the one who could get anything running, rig a security system out of spare parts, make a working firearm out of three broken rifles, and get us home despite a busted GPS unit. I was the guy who fixed things and helped get my team home safe and sound, mission accomplished."

Sophie found it difficult to think of him as part of a team when he so adamantly held himself apart from everyone except his son. But that didn't really matter under the circumstances, did it?

"Can you fix this?" she asked, meaning the situation, and the threat that might or might not hang over them, depending on whether the bomber was still at Lonesome Lake.

It was a long moment before he said, "I can't promise you that nothing bad is going to happen to us, Sophie. But I can and will promise to do everything I can to get us both out of here in one piece."

It wasn't a simple, easy answer, but she wouldn't have believed him if he'd gone with simple or easy. Because he'd gone with honesty instead, she took a deep breath to settle the nervous quiver in her stomach, and told herself that would have to be good enough. She nodded. "Okay. What's next?" She shot a look at the generator, which had settled into a good working rhythm of engine noise. "Do we need to find fuel?"

"The generators draw from a pair of underground tanks, and the building inspector said they checked out fine. I had them topped up before construction started, so we should be all set in that department." He didn't say "unless someone has tampered with them," but she knew they were both thinking it. He continued, "Now that the generator is running, let's go back inside and test the lights. If the power is still off, we'll head for the basement and check the electrical panel."

She offered the .45. "Take this. You know what to do with it. I don't."

He took the weapon without comment, tucking it beneath the parka, at the small of his back. The small action bore the ease of familiarity, which she found both reassuring and unsettling. It was reassuring in that it made her feel that much safer, knowing he was armed. Yet it was unsettling in that it kindled a core of warmth in the pit of her stomach. Apparently, she was turned on by a guy with a gun. Who knew?

Then again, odds were it wasn't the gun. It was Griffin. Had been from the first moment they'd met.

He glanced at her and lifted an eyebrow. "Ready to brave the elements?"

Ignoring the dangerous warmth of an attraction she had no business feeling, even though they were in a situation and place far out of their normal reality, she pulled her parka more securely around her body, and nodded. "Ready as I'll ever be."

The storm slapped at them the moment he slid open the door of the generator shed, but she was more or less braced for the blizzard's fury this time. Hanging on to each other, they slogged across the short distance to the mansion entrance without incident.

Once they were back inside, though, their luck ran out.

When Griffin tested the power, nothing happened.

"Damn it." He jiggled the switch, checked that the overhead chandelier had bulbs, then tried another nearby. Still nothing. "The wiring in here looks complete. Let's hope we just need to flip some circuit breakers."

"Basement it is, then," Sophie said, though the idea dragged at her.

She was running out of steam fast; they'd skipped out on the food she'd prepared, and she tended to weaken quickly when her blood sugar got low. Add to that the bumps and bruises from the accident on the bridge, and the overall drain of the stress and the cold, and she was just about done in. Not that she was going to admit any such thing to Griffin. *Probation*, she reminded herself. *You need this job.*

Oddly, the mantra didn't work nearly as well as it had earlier in the day. Maybe it was because she was tired, maybe because of the threat of danger, but she found herself needing an added incentive to keep going. *Don't give up*, she told herself. *Don't let Griffin down.*

And yeah, she knew it was skirting close to the edge of stupidity, venturing too near that closed-off part of her brain where she put impossible things, but she'd had a hard day. She'd give herself a pass this time.

They headed back across the huge house, stopping at a solid-paneled door. Griffin swung it open to reveal a stairwell that led down into darkness. The blackness and the faintly stale smell coming from the basement raised the fine hairs on the back of Sophie's neck, but when Griffin glanced at her as if asking whether she was all set, she nodded. It was just a basement, after all.

Still, she was comforted to see him draw the .45 and hold it cross-handed with the flashlight as he played the light over what they could see of the basement from the top of the stairs. The steps ended in a smooth cement floor, where, inexplicably, someone had placed a woven mat that had the word *Welcome* imprinted on it. The rest of the space immediately surrounding the stairwell was clear, looking almost swept clean.

"Seems harmless enough," Griffin muttered, more to himself than to her.

Sophie followed him down the stairs, trying not to crowd too close. Although the area immediately surrounding the stairs was clear, the basement itself proved to be a labyrinthine maze of pylons and load-bearing cement-block walls designed to support the massive weight of the mansion. The supports divided the space into a series of interconnecting rooms that proved to be empty and echoing, and nearly identical to one another. Within minutes, Sophie questioned whether she would be able to find her way out again. Faint light came from narrow windows set near the ceiling, the snow-filtered illumination casting the scene with a strange blue glow.

"What is this place?" she whispered.

Griffin lifted a shoulder. "The Realtor said the previous owner used it for storage. Given who that owner turned out to be, I'm not taking any bets."

She suppressed a shiver. "How do you know we're going the right way?"

"The panel's in the northwest corner of the building, which is the side sunk into the mountain," he answered, as though that should explain everything. Which it might have, if Sophie had ever needed to think of things in terms of north and west. As it was, she'd lived pretty much her entire life within a hundred-mile radius of San Fran, and knew how to get where she was going without a compass.

Gritting her teeth, knowing that was no excuse, she started counting doorways and turns, and scuffing her feet in the thin layer of dust that had accumulated in some of the doorway corners, marking the way they'd come in. Not because she thought Griffin was likely to abandon her, but because it was something active she could do, and made her feel as though she was taking an iota of control.

Eventually, they came through a doorway and found themselves in a larger space, where two outer structural walls joined in a right-angle corner. Two other doorways led off along the main walls, leading to darkness beyond. Griffin flashed his light on a large gray box that was bolted onto the wall and had a profusion of wires and conduits running into and out of it. The door of the electrical panel hung open, revealing rows of circuit breakers, all of them in the off position.

"Now there's some good news," Griffin said, heading for the panel. "If we just flip the breakers, we should have lights and—"

A blur erupted from the darkened doorway to their left. Sophie turned, gasping at the sight of a man in jeans and a heavy parka. He wore a knit cap pulled down low over his brow and a muffler up over his chin, so only his cold blue eyes were visible, and then only for the split second it took her to focus on the heavy crowbar he held in leather-gloved hands.

"Griffin!" she screamed as the man raised the crowbar and swung it straight at her head.

Chapter Five

Griffin lunged for Sophie's attacker, not stopping to think or plan, his only goal to get the bastard away from her. He deflected the crowbar with his forearm, ignored the searing pain of impact, and drove his shoulder into the other man's chest.

The tackle sent the men sprawling through the nearest doorway into darkness. Griffin had lost his flashlight, but belatedly realized he'd kept hold of the .45. He brought it to bear just as the other man jabbed at him with the crowbar, digging the tip in to his ribs.

Griffin's breath whooshed out. He grabbed the end of the crowbar with his free hand, preventing a followthrough blow, but didn't dare start shooting. Not with the two of them sandwiched together on a cement surface, and ricochet an all-too-real possibility.

"Take this," he called to Sophie, and sent the weapon skidding in her direction. He didn't hear an answer, which wasn't a good sign. Had the bastard gotten her with the crowbar?

Rage spiked alongside the fighting adrenaline that

had Griffin's blood hammering in his veins. He might not be that young, brash marine who'd taken out the enemy on his CO's orders anymore, but he wasn't the staid businessman, either. He was both of those men, and something in between—someone smarter and more controlled, yet willing to kill in order to protect.

Roaring a curse, he twisted out from underneath his heavily muscled attacker and fought to rip the crowbar from the other man's hands. The men wrestled, grunting curses, landing elbows and knees as they struggled in the darkness. Searing pain exploded in Griffin's upper arm, but he didn't let go. He dragged himself to his feet, fighting for leverage.

Suddenly, his opponent released the crowbar and jumped back. Overbalancing, Griffin crashed to the side with a yell. He blinked against the pain, and too late, saw a bare fist coming his way. He tried to duck the punch, caught the blow on his temple, and sagged, dazed.

"Get away from him!" Sophie shouted. She aimed the .45 and pulled the trigger. The gun roared, and the other man cried out in pain, grabbing at his right side.

Griffin lunged and snagged the other man's coat, grunting as the pain in his arm slashed to agony. His adversary yanked away and bolted, getting through the far doorway a split second before Sophie's next shot slammed into the wall nearby and pinged with a dangerous ricochet.

"Cease fire!" Griffin shouted, ducking.

When the gunshot echo faded, he could hear the sound of running footsteps, followed by a grating noise.

Then there was nothing but the sound of rapid, rasping breaths. Griffin's own. Sophie's.

"Are you okay?" he asked, fighting to marshal his breathing and not let on that his right arm was rapidly going numb. The bastard hadn't had a knife, so Griffin had to assume he'd been nailed with the crowbar and hadn't noticed immediately in the heat of battle. It happened that way sometimes.

"I think…" Her quivering voice trailed off, and he heard her take a deep breath. When she spoke again, her tone was steady, if weak. "I think I shot him."

"I think so, too."

Something in his voice must've tipped her off, because she turned, clicked on her flashlight and shone it on him. "You're hurt." Dull horror filled her tone. "I didn't shoot you, too, did I?"

"No. Guy nailed me in the shoulder with the crowbar. I don't think anything's broken." The last was a lie meant to reassure them both, because even if it was broken, there wasn't much they could do about it. And he was right-handed. If he lost full use of that arm, it would seriously limit their defensive options, which were going to become crucial now that they knew for sure they weren't alone in the mansion.

Sophie's voice carried a fine tremor of nerves—or maybe incipient hysteria—when she said, "We should get you back to the apartment and take a look at it."

"You're okay?" he asked again, needing to be sure. "He didn't get you with the crowbar? I thought he might've hit you in that first rush."

"No." She shook her head. "But after he missed me, he took a swing at the fuse box before you got to him."

Griffin took one look at the electrical panel, and cursed bitterly. The thing was a write-off. No fuses meant no power to the apartment, and no juice he could use to rig pieces of the old security system into something that would protect them from their attacker.

A warning bell sounded at the back of Griffin's brain, because taking out the bridge and the electricals smacked of military strategy. Or the work of a professional.

"Come on. Let's see if we can follow the bastard." Griffin retrieved his flashlight from where it had fallen during the fight, clicked it on, and sent the beam skimming down the dim corridor where their attacker had disappeared.

"Did you recognize him?" Sophie asked, joining him as he moved along the corridor. "Was it Perry?"

"Not sure. Could've been." The man's face had been obscured. His height had been about right, but that didn't mean much.

The hallway floor was clean—maybe too clean?— providing little in the way of evidence. Griffin found a couple of drops of blood, but absolutely no sign of where their attacker had gone, how he'd disappeared. It was a mystery.

Nodding to the weapon Sophie held at the ready, Griffin said, "At least we've still got the gun. I'd guess we're one-up on him in that department given that he used a damned crowbar as a—" He broke off as he realized something.

"What is it?" Sophie said quickly. "What's wrong?"

It wasn't what was wrong, he knew. It was that something had finally gone their way. Maybe. "We need to bring the crowbar back with us, but wrap it in something before you touch it."

"Why not?"

A grim smile touched his face as he remembered the sight of an incoming fist. A *bare* fist. "The bastard lost one of his gloves during the fight. He must've grabbed it when he left, but I had the crowbar, so he couldn't take that. If he left a usable fingerprint, and we can find some way to get an image of it over to the CSU, Martinez's people should be able to tell us who we're dealing with."

"That's assuming the prints are on file."

"Perry was in the army. He'll be in the armed forces database." And Vince Del Gardo would be in AFIS, Griffin knew, but he didn't want to voice that alternative if he could help it.

The idea of being stalked by a contractor in self-defense mode was bad enough. He didn't want to think how much worse things could get if it turned out that their enemy was a cold-blooded fugitive.

WHEN THEY GOT BACK to the apartment, Griffin checked inside and out for signs that their attacker had been there. When he found no signs of tampering, he hid the crowbar—which might or might not hold valuable evidence—and went back outside the apartment to string the rope and scrap metal at strategic points in the hallway. Once he was done with that, he braved the storm to do the same outside the windows.

All the while, Sophie followed him with the .45, watching his back. She hated the weight of the weapon, and the faint smell that clung to it, and to her. Intellectually, she knew she'd done the right thing, that she hadn't had an option other than shooting the man. But that didn't stop her from replaying the moment over and over again in her head, feeling the kick of recoil and hearing his cry of pain. She couldn't stop seeing the blood trail in her mind's eye, and knowing she'd been the one to cause it.

That knowledge dragged her down, and had her close to tears by the time Griffin finally finished, and declared the apartment safe. They both knew he meant, "as safe as I can get it under the circumstances."

Mindful of his injured arm, which he favored when he thought she wasn't looking, she packed several large snowballs and piled them just outside the apartment door, figuring the main house was close enough to freezing that they'd stay frozen. They wouldn't last as long as an icepack, but they'd be better than nothing.

Back inside the apartment, they went around to each of the rooms to draw all the curtains and pull the shades, closing out the world. The four-room space was warm from the fire, and orange and yellow light played from the mismatched candles and the kerosene lanterns as the early storm dusk turned to full dark.

Under other circumstances, Sophie knew, it might've been a scene set for romance. Under the present circumstances, she felt vulnerable and exposed. Their enemy had used explosives once before, what was to say he wouldn't do the same again?

As if she'd said the words aloud, Griffin crossed to her, gripped her shoulder and squeezed it in a gesture of support. "If he had the means to attack us in here, he would've done it already. Besides, he's wounded. He'll need tonight at least to deal with the injury."

Because that thought was both reassuring and disquieting, she changed the subject. "How's your arm?"

He rotated it, then grimaced. "It's pretty sore," he admitted. "And my fingers are tingling."

She pointed to the bathroom. "In there, shirt off. Let's see what we're dealing with."

That gave him pause. "You've got medical training?"

"I can hold my own in the first-aid department," she said evasively, having no wish to discuss the decade-plus she'd spent becoming an expert in home health care, when her mother's medical problems had rendered her practically bedridden, yet the doctors they'd been able to afford weren't able—and frankly didn't care enough—to provide a solid diagnosis or useful treatment suggestions.

Griffin held her gaze for a long moment, as though asking if she was sure this was a good idea.

She raised an eyebrow. "Shy?"

He snorted. "Not hardly."

"Then get in the bathroom and strip, boss." She said it that way in an effort to be funny, and also to remind herself of their respective roles.

Still, there was a hum of warmth in her core and an unfamiliar beat in her blood as she followed him into the apartment's single bathroom, which was done in the same neutrals in the main room, with splashes of color in the southwestern-themed towels and a touch of femininity in a soapstone bowl of potpourri beside the sink.

Sophie turned her back on Griffin and busied herself looking in the medicine cabinet for painkillers at the very least. All the while, she was acutely aware of Griffin's presence filling the small room, and the rustle of movement and hiss of pain as he pulled off his borrowed shirt and sweater.

The medicine cabinet yielded ibuprofen, as well as an arnica cream that would help take the sting out of any bruising, and help speed the healing process. That was assuming it was a bruise. If he'd broken or cracked the bone, there was little she could do beyond stabilizing the spot and telling him to use it as little as possible, which wasn't really feasible given their situation.

And she was stalling, she knew.

Taking a deep breath, she swung shut the mirrored door of the medicine cabinet, which then gave her a clear view of her own flushed face, and the half-naked man standing behind her.

If she'd ever consciously wondered whether the delicious golden undertones of his skin were from the sun, her question was answered now in glorious expanse of gold-burnished skin that stretched across his powerful chest. Since she knew he wasn't one to lie out and work on a meticulous tan, she could only assume he looked like that all over his body. Which was a thought she absolutely, positively shouldn't have, and one that stuck in her mind and echoed in the heat that chased through her veins, even as she noticed the angry red spot on his upper arm. The burgeoning mark was already turning purplish-black, suggesting that it was a deep bruise, maybe something worse.

His eyes met hers in the mirror. "You sure this is a good idea?"

It was as close as either of them had come to admitting that there was a bite of chemistry between them. Or rather, that there was a great big ravening gulp of chemistry, at least on her part.

But she nodded. "I don't like the looks of that bruise. No offense, but I'll feel far better if you have full use of both arms."

"And you can help with that?"

"I'll do my best." She turned around finally, so they were face-to-face, and she forced herself to drop into the caretaker's role that was all too familiar. She directed him to sit on the closed toilet lid, and moved in to inspect the damage the crowbar had done to the flesh and muscle of his upper arm.

She didn't stare at his broad chest, or let her eyes follow the faint trail of masculine hair that dusted across his pecs and led downward, disappearing into the waistband of his borrowed jeans. Instead, she kept herself busy and businesslike, testing his grip and range of motion, and probing at the edges of the bruise, then using the snowballs from out in the hallway to ice the injury and bring the swelling down as far as she could.

All the while, she was acutely aware of the warmth of his skin, and the heat that seemed to be pouring off his body and curling inside hers.

Griffin stared straight ahead, his jaw locked.

"I'm pretty sure it's just a bruise," she said finally, "though the word 'just' probably feels relative from where you're sitting. I bet it hurts like hell."

"It doesn't tickle," he said, and flicked a glance at her. She saw reflected heat in his eyes, and felt an answering flare within her. But his voice was cool and casual when he said, "Where'd you pick up the medical stuff?"

"I spent some time looking after a family member," she answered vaguely. She handed him the ibuprofen. "Take these—no more than four to start with, then two every couple of hours. It should keep the pain down to a dull roar." She reached for the arnica cream and squeezed some into her palm. "This'll help, too."

"What is it?"

"Arnica. It takes out the sting and helps speed healing." Seeing that he didn't look convinced, she said, "It works. Trust me."

"I do trust you," he said, and then looked surprised to have said it. Trying to cover whatever slip he'd just made, he kicked up the corner of his mouth and said, "You haven't dumped any scalding liquids on me in a while, after all."

He had a point, she realized. Whatever she was feeling right then, it wasn't nerves. At least not the kind that made her clumsy. More like the kind that brought a flush to her skin and a spin to her head, and made her want to step toward him rather than away. She was too close to him already, standing behind him and to the side, where she had easy access to his injured arm, and entirely too good a view of his broad, muscular back. She couldn't make herself move away, though, held transfixed by the intimacy that had grown between them over the course of the day, whether either of them wanted to acknowledge it.

He'd saved her life down by the bridge, and fought to protect her just now in the basement. She'd guarded his back and helped him when his reserves finally gave out. They weren't the same people they'd been that morning when they'd gotten on the plane, planning on spending the night at their respective homes in San Fran.

Instead they'd be spending the night at Lonesome Lake, together by candlelight.

"Go ahead," he said, turning slightly away from her so she could apply the cream. "You're the doctor."

She complied wordlessly, unable to come up with anything witty, or even mildly intelligent, to say. First, she smeared the arnica gel along his heavy shoulder muscle, then worked it down to where his bicep joined. There, in the natural indentation that was so much more defined than she would've imagined in a man she thought of as having a desk job, was where the worst of the bruising had bloomed.

"This is probably going to hurt," she warned.

He said nothing, simply waited. Knowing there was no

use putting it off, she started working the gel in to his skin, turning the application into a light massage that would break up some of the bruising as it formed, and help the medication get to the damaged tissues more easily. As she did so, she told herself this was no different from easing the aches and pains that had plagued her mother's joints for so long. Only it was very, very different.

She loved the feel of his skin beneath her fingertips, and the warmth of his body up close. She reveled in the leashed strength of his muscles, and fought not to inhale his spicy, male scent.

And, she realized, she needed to stop it, right now.

Griffin wasn't hers, wouldn't ever be hers, and to think otherwise was just foolishness. They were in an artificially intimate situation. It wouldn't do her any good to create unrealistic fantasies out of it.

Dropping her hands, she took a big step back, away from him. "And, um, that's pretty much it. Keep up with the ibuprofen, and you should feel a big improvement by morning."

He didn't meet her eyes, just kept staring straight ahead. "Thanks. I owe you one."

"I'll, um, go reheat our lunch," she said. "Which I guess is dinner now." But she didn't move.

"Okay." He didn't move, either. At least she didn't think he did. But if that was the case, how come it seemed that they were closer to each other than they'd been before?

Then, abruptly, he stood and moved past her, stalking out of the bathroom into the main room of the apartment. She didn't follow, didn't think her legs would support her just then if she'd tried. In fact, she stayed in the bathroom until she heard him opening dresser drawers, looking for another shirt in the bedroom.

Relieved to avoid facing him just then, she escaped to the kitchen, and went through the motions of reheating the food from earlier, clicking on the propane stove, and stirring in some condensed milk when the macaroni and cheese looked less than appetizing the second time around.

"We could toss it and make something else," Griffin suggested from very close behind her.

Sophie jolted. She hadn't realized he'd come into the kitchen, hadn't realized he was so near, practically looking over her shoulder.

Steeling herself to ignore the warmth that kindled in her blood at his proximity, she shot him a look. "Spoken like a man who's never had to make a box of Kraft stretch a couple of days."

"Try one who can't remember the last time he ate anything that came solely from a box and a couple of cans, finished off with a side of tap water."

"Right." She nodded and concentrated on stirring the noodles so they wouldn't stick. "You probably grew up in a place like this is going to be once the renovations are finished. A mansion with three pools, a cook and a live-in nanny." As soon as the words came out, she regretted them. It'd sounded more like an accusation than an observation, and it was seriously none of her business either way. "Sorry," she said, a beat too late. "If it's all the same to you, I'd appreciate it if you'd pretend I didn't just say that."

He didn't respond for a moment, just stood there too close to her. She didn't dare turn, didn't dare look at him. She wasn't even entirely sure what she was afraid of seeing in his eyes, whether it was his potential for anger that had her nerves humming…or something else entirely.

After a pause that seemed like it went on forever, he moved away from her and sat at the small table on the other side of the eat-in kitchen. For a few seconds she was relieved, thinking he'd taken her at her word and was pretending she hadn't just sniped at him for being born into a wealthy family, when she'd grown up in anything but.

Then he said, "No nannies or cooks, actually. My dad and my Uncle Will started VaughnTec when I was ten, maybe eleven, trying to get in on the early wave of VCR technology. They went with the beta format, which never caught on, and it was pretty much like that for them all along. They had the right ideas, but they were always a little too late, or sank their money down the wrong R & D path."

Don't pry, Sophie told herself firmly as she dished up for both of them. "Yet no dinners out of boxes."

"My mom cooked," he said simply. "She cooked, she gardened, she wrote poetry…and she made life fun. She was younger than my dad, and very different in temperament, but somehow they were the perfect match." He paused, and though she hadn't asked, said, "She and my dad died six years ago in a car accident. It was one of those things—a big rig blew a tire and swerved…and that was it."

Sophie hesitated in the midst of setting their soup bowls out on the table, then forced herself to keep moving. She set out the last of the food, then sat opposite him and picked up her spoon before she said, "I'm sorry."

Because really, what else was there to say? She didn't know him well enough to suggest he should be grateful for having had a steady nuclear family for so long, didn't have the right to lay that on him just because a streak of nasty jealousy had reared up at the thought of a mother who cooked, gardened and wrote poetry, never mind the thought of childhood being fun.

Those were her problems, not his.

He nodded. "Thanks." He dug into his soup, then gestured with his spoon. "What, no quid pro quo? Not going to tell me why you're an expert at minimizing bruises and resuscitating macaroni and cheese? Nice job on both of those things, by the way."

"Thanks. And no, I think I'll skip the life-story portion of today's entertainment."

That had him putting down his spoon and giving her his full attention, which was exactly what she'd been hoping to avoid. "And she continues to surprise me," he said as though in an aside to himself. To her, he said, "Most of the women I've had occasion to share a meal with would've jumped at the chance to tell me all about their lives."

"Then I guess I'm not like those women."

"No," he said, drawing out the word reflectively. "No, you're not."

He picked up his spoon again and kept eating, and for a few minutes they sat in companionable silence. Just when Sophie was starting to relax, though, he said, "So tell me something else about yourself. What do you really want to do with your life?" He held up a hand to forestall her immediate defensive response. "Let me re-phrase, because obviously the PC answer is 'be your executive assistant for ever and ever, Griffin.' If you could do anything at all, if money were no object and you had all the time in the world, what would you do?"

"I'd become a lawyer," she said, the words popping out before she was aware that she'd decided to share that unrealistic dream. "Then, since you said money was no object, I'd become an advocate. I'd help low-income single parents and marginal families fight for proper medical coverage, and—" She broke off, knowing she'd already revealed too much on the "story of my life" front. She lifted a shoulder. "And that's it. If I won the lottery or whatever."

Needing badly to move, she popped up from her chair and started clearing the table.

Griffin rose when she did, and reached for her plate. "You cooked. I should clean up."

"You realize there's no hot water, right? No electricity, no dishwasher."

"I'll manage."

She was tempted, but in the end waved him off. "You go on. Call your son and then rest your arm. Something tells me that tomorrow could be a very long day." She paused, suddenly gripped by the knowledge that they couldn't really think about tomorrow until they'd made it through the night, and there were no guarantees on that front. "What are we going to do?" she finally asked, unable to keep her voice from going thin.

"The best we can," he said, which wasn't really an answer, but was somehow calming nonetheless. After a moment, he continued, "I truly do believe he'll lay low tonight, though I'll walk the perimeter every hour or so, and I sleep very lightly, so if anything hits the trip wires, I'll know it. As for tomorrow…" He trailed off. Shrugged. "Let's get some sleep and see what the day brings, okay?"

She nodded. "You're the boss."

He left the kitchen, taking one of the kerosene lanterns with him, and she puttered in the kitchen far longer than she needed to, stalling. By the time she finally made it out into the main room, he was off the phone and sprawled out on the sofa cushions, which he'd laid out end-to-end near the fireplace, where it was warmest. He was fully clothed, and his boots were close at hand.

What was more, he'd carried the mattress out of the bedroom, into the living room, and set it up on the other side of the fireplace.

Sophie stopped dead, staring at it.

"Don't freak," he said without moving or opening his eyes. "It's not an indecent proposal. If we have to move fast for whatever reason, I don't want to lose time going into the bedroom after you."

She stared at the mattress a moment longer, then nodded. "Of course. No problem." But as she got ready for bed, copying him by staying clothed and keeping her boots within reach, she wondered what he would do if she gave him another piece of her life story, namely that this would be the first time she'd ever slept with a man. Literally or figuratively.

She lay down and stared into the fire, expecting that her racing brain would keep her wide awake. Instead, soothed by the regular sound of his breathing, the crackle of the fire, and even the howl of the storm winds outside, she drifted off.

A HALF A MILE AWAY, deep in the hidden tunnel system that bracketed the mansion and a large portion of the estate, the bald man leaned against the rocky tunnel wall and shone a flashlight on the hole the bitch had blown in his side.

It was deep and ugly, flushed red at the margins, and it hurt like the devil. His head was spinning from the loss of blood, and he was too disoriented to make another try for his targets tonight. He needed rest and fluids. Then, when he was feeling steadier, he'd be back on the hunt.

Griffin Vaughn and his secretary might've gotten lucky a second time, but their luck would run out soon enough. And then they'd be dead.

Chapter Six

Sophie slept deeply, not even surfacing all the way when, every few hours, Griffin rose, pulled on his boots, and checked the perimeter he'd set up around the apartment.

Each time when he returned, he reassured her in a low voice, telling her there was no sign of anyone out there. Then he tossed another log or two on the fire, keeping the room toasty warm. By the time he'd returned to his pallet, she'd dropped back to sleep.

When she finally came all the way awake, it was tough to tell at first whether it was morning or not, because the room was still dark, so she climbed up off the mattress and crossed to the window. Pushing the drape aside a bit, she peered out into a leaden gray world of whipping ice and wind.

It was morning, and the storm definitely hadn't broken.

"Sorry," Griffin said from his side of the room, his voice thick with sleep. "I don't think we're getting out of here today."

No matter how many times she'd told herself that the sheriff was probably right, that the blizzard would last another day at least, a knot of disappointment tightened in her gut, wrapping itself around the ball of fear that said the next time they went up against their enemy, they might not be as lucky as they'd been so far.

Worrying about it, though, wasn't going to help. She needed to do something more productive, more active.

"Go back to sleep," she told Griffin, knowing he hadn't gotten much actual rest during the night. "I'll wake you if I hear anything."

He muttered something that she thought was assent, and settled back into his makeshift bed. Forcing herself not to watch him sleep, or think the things she shouldn't be thinking in the light of day, she headed for the kitchen and started coffee. While it brewed, she powered up her PDA and placed a call to Sheriff Martinez.

"Martinez here," the sheriff answered.

"Sheriff, it's Sophie. We've had some developments up here." She briefly outlined what had happened the night before, ending with: "So that confirms it. Whoever is up here with us wants us out of the way."

There was a long pause as the sheriff digested the new information. After a moment, he said, "Can you give me a description?"

"Sorry, not really. Average height and weight, jeans and a parka, and he was wearing a hat and had a scarf wrapped around his face, so I couldn't see anything. The light wasn't good, either." She paused, holding onto their one thin hope. "Here's the thing. He was wearing gloves when he first attacked us, but he lost one of them during the fight."

"You've got the glove?"

"No. But we've got the crowbar, and Griffin is pretty sure the guy grabbed on to it with his bare hand. He thinks it's worth checking out, anyway."

"I would agree wholeheartedly if it weren't for this damned storm," Martinez said irritably. "It's got us completely shut down here. The Del Gardo investigation is at a standstill, and with every inch of snow that falls, we're losing crucial evidence at our various crime scenes. It's a bloody mess down here. Which, I know, doesn't help you and Griffin one bit. But that's where I'm at."

Thinking of what Griffin had said, Sophie asked, "Is there, I don't know, some way we could process the prints ourselves and e-mail you some pictures?"

Martinez muttered a curse, then said, "Sorry, that was aimed at me, not you. I got so caught up in thinking about the storm and being frustrated that I can't get anyone up there to help you, that I wasn't thinking outside the box. Let me transfer you to the KCCU. You're going to be talking to one of the best we've got, investigator Callie MacBride. Okay?"

"Yes. Thanks so much."

"Keep in touch. And be careful."

On one hand Sophie was pleased the sheriff had stopped doing the "don't scare the pretty, very young-looking lady" routine. On the other, she suspected it was because he was out of options. Which wasn't a very encouraging thought.

Sophie heard a couple of clicks on the line, and then a soft beep and the phone on the other end started to ring. Moments later, the line went live and a crisp, businesslike female voice said, "Crime scene unit. This is Callie MacBride."

Sophie introduced herself and explained the situation, trying to keep it to just the facts—partly because she instinctively sensed that the investigator was both busy and to-the-point, and also because she was a little afraid that if she let the emotions seep in, she'd lose her cool completely. She finished by repeating the request she'd made of Sheriff Martinez, for help lifting the fingerprints and seeing if they could ID their attacker long-distance.

When she was done, there was a long, drawn-out silence on the other end of the phone. Then Callie's voice came back, much softer than it'd been before. "You poor thing. I can see why Patrick—that's Sheriff Martinez—is about killing himself trying to figure out a way to get you and Vaughn down off the mountain."

Sophie's voice shook a little when she said, "Can you help with the fingerprints? I think…I think it'd be better if we knew who we're up against."

"Yes, I think we can do something. What I'm actually going to do is have you call Ava Wright. She's a forensic specialist who's also working on the Del Gardo case. Her knowledge base is a little more esoteric than mine, so I think she'll have a better idea of what household powders might work to provide the detail we're going to need." Callie recited the other woman's number.

"Got it. Thanks."

"Good luck, Sophie."

Ava Wright picked up on the first ring, and Sophie

described the situation. Ava proved to be a warmer, bubblier version of Callie, and made Sophie feel as though she and Ava had been friends for some time. Ava talked her through the fingerprinting procedure and suggested some kitchen and bathroom items that might serve as fingerprinting powders.

After they were done discussing the actual lifting protocol and what Sophie should use to provide sufficient contrast for the photographs she planned to take using her PDA, Ava sighed and said, "For your sake I really hope it's not Del Gardo. I know Patrick is dead set against it being Perry, since they know each other some, but at the same time, I'd say your hunky ex-marine is probably a better match for an ex-army contractor than a mob boss."

"My hunky ex-marine," Sophie repeated, suddenly thinking of all that golden skin, and the feel of warm man and muscle beneath her fingertips.

"I researched him on the Internet, found some society-type pictures. Nice. Might not be much of a hardship being snowed in with a guy like him." Ava paused, as if inviting gossip. When Sophie didn't say anything, she continued, "Then again, he's your boss, right? You probably don't want to go there, huh?"

"I…I don't know what to say," Sophie confessed. "Do you need to know this for the case?"

"Nope, just being nosy. Pregnant woman's prerogative." Ava paused and her voice went soft. "And you sound like you could use someone to talk to."

Sophie choked up and nodded, which was silly

because Ava couldn't see a nod through the phone. So she managed to say, "Thanks. I...thanks."

"You go ahead and try those prints now, okay? Call me if you need help. Or even if you just need to talk. And remember, you and the hunka-hunka might be on your own up there at the mansion, but there are a whole bunch of us down here worried about you, and pulling for you, and trying to figure out some way to get to you. You're not alone in this. Okay?"

"Okay," Sophie whispered into the phone, as a fat tear trickled down her cheek. "Thank you."

Once she'd hung up and powered down the PDA, she just sat there at the kitchen table for a long moment, soaking in the feeling of community, which was something she'd never really experienced in San Fran, though she'd lived there her entire life. Maybe it was because she'd spent so much of her time dealing with her mother's illness, or maybe she herself had never made enough of an effort, but even in the neighborhood where she'd grown up, she'd always felt like an outsider looking in. Yet in the space of a single day, the cops of Kenner County had accepted her more warmly, and were worried about her more deeply than anyone back home ever had.

It's because of Griffin, a small inner voice said sourly. *You've got to be rich in order to get attention in this world.* And maybe that was true, but for the moment she was simply grateful that Patrick Martinez, Callie MacBride and Ava Wright were on her side.

"Okay." She drew a deep breath and scrubbed both hands across her face. "Time to get to work."

Energized by the thought of doing something useful, she searched the kitchen and bathroom, and assembled a likely-looking collection of spices, makeup and talcum powder, along with clear packing tape and paper in several different dark colors, in addition to plain white. She completed her kit with a worn-looking blusher brush that was the closest she could come to the fine, natural-bristled paintbrush Ava had recommended.

Throughout it all, Griffin slept deeply, apparently trusting her to rouse him if there was any sign of trouble.

Figuring she should practice first, she pulled down a pair of juice glasses, gripping them tightly with her fingertips to make prints. Then she got to work, starting with cinnamon and working from there.

Ten minutes later she had a halfway decent lift of one of her own fingerprints, in blusher on black paper. Holding her breath, she powered up the PDA and used it to photograph the print. It worked.

Her heart was tapping at her ribs as she retrieved the parka-wrapped crowbar. Holding her breath, hoping against hope that this would give them some answers, she bent over the crowbar and started dusting. An hour later, she had twenty lifted prints. She could see that some were the same, some were different. The best part was that she thought she had three thumbs. Even if two were Griffin's, the other one should—maybe?—belong to their assailant.

Blood humming with excitement, she photographed the prints, then scrolled down the list of recently connected numbers to call Ava back. It wasn't until the second ring that she looked at the display and checked the number.

It wasn't Ava's local number. She'd missed and hit the wrong redial.

Sophie groaned when she recognized Griffin's home number in San Francisco. She'd scrolled down too far, darn it! And the call put her in an awkward situation, because Griffin had made it very clear that his home and family were off-limits to her under any but the most extreme circumstances. And while the current situation was certainly dire, it had nothing to do with Darryn and Luke.

By then, though, it was too late to disconnect, because someone was already picking up.

"That you, Griffin?" a pleasant, male voice said.

"Sorry, no. It's Sophie. Is this Darryn?"

"That'd be me," the male nanny agreed cheerfully, but then his tone changed to one of concern. "Everything okay out there?"

She paused, because she didn't have a clue how to answer. She'd only met Darryn once, when Griffin had asked her to stop by his house and pick up an important document. On first impression, Darryn was a warm, fun-loving guy who'd taken a break from college to, as he called it, "get my beer goggles off and figure out what I want to be when I grow up." In the space of maybe two minutes, she'd also learned that he was a cousin of Griffin's, removed a time or two, and had gladly taken on the offered role of childcare to Luke, because, as Darryn had said, the job gave him breathing room, and both Griffin and Luke were "cool dudes."

The meeting had been brief, but Sophie had come away liking Griffin's cousin very much. She'd also gotten a glimpse of three-year-old Luke, who had popped his head around the corner just as she was leaving. The boy's short, blond hair and shy smile had tugged at her, as had his wide-eyed stare. But when Griffin had sent her over to the house, he'd made it clear—not in so many words, of course, but clear nonetheless—that she was part of his business life, not his home life, and should get herself in and out with a minimum of chitchat. He'd softened the order by admitting that Luke missed Kathleen, and he didn't want the child to get too attached to her replacement. Sophie suspected there was more to it than that, but hadn't pressed, because really, Griffin's home life was none of her business.

Mindful of that, she didn't answer Darryn's question directly, instead saying, "I'm sorry, but this is actually a wrong number. I scrolled down too far and pulled up this number from when Griffin called you guys last night."

"He wanted us to know you two would be stuck for a few days. Said for me to have the helicopter at the closest flyable airport, ready to buzz in and pick you guys up the moment the storm breaks, because otherwise it'll be a few days more before the roads are clear."

"That's about the sum of it," Sophie said, lying through her teeth, because Griffin obviously hadn't wanted his cousin or son to worry about the full extent of the problems up at Lonesome Lake. "Sorry to bother you with the misdial."

"No prob. You going to call your family now?" Darryn asked, apparently in no rush to get off the phone.

What family? she thought, feeling the lack with a sharper pang than usual. "Nope, it's all business. I need to follow up on something we've got going on down here."

Darryn groaned theatrically. "Dude, I know how that is. Or rather, I know how Griffin is. The man's a total workaholic. Do me a favor and talk him into making a snowman or going sledding or something. The guy could use a snow day."

"I'll do that," Sophie said, which was a total lie. Even if they'd simply been stuck together in a snowstorm, she couldn't picture herself talking Griffin into anything, much less something as frivolous as a toboggan run or a snow angel. Pushing aside a quick, wistful image of doing just that, she said, "I'm sure he'll call you himself later. Bye."

She was about to scroll back to Ava's number and make her call when something drew her attention to the doorway—a noise, maybe, or the sort of sixth sense she seemed to be developing when it came to her boss, a preternatural awareness of where he was, and what sort of mood he was in.

Nerves shimmered to life, running in fine currents just beneath her skin. Sure enough, when she looked over, she found Griffin standing in the doorway, staring at her, his expression unreadable.

His hair was wet, his skin pale, suggesting that he'd taken a cold shower. Where the beginnings of beard stubble had humanized him the day before, now his strong jawline was clean-shaven, making him look more like the businessman she'd been working for than the rougher, more down-to-earth soldier she'd started getting to know the day before. The change created a distance, putting them back to boss and assistant rather than two people working together in an effort to survive.

He looked pointedly at the phone. "Talking to Darryn?"

"Sorry. I scrolled down too far and hit your number rather than the KCCU's. Then I didn't want to worry Darryn by hanging up."

Griffin's eyes didn't warm. If anything, they chilled further. "Long conversation for a wrong number."

Irritation prickled. "I thought you'd want him to think everything was okay here. So, yes, I chatted for a minute rather than telling him I had to hang up right away and call the Kenner County CSU because I wanted to send them some fingerprints that might belong to the guy who's been trying to kill us."

He glanced at the kitchen table, which was littered with the leftovers from her fingerprinting project, along with the sheets of black construction paper on which she'd affixed the lifted prints. He nodded shortly. "Good work. Get those to the CSU pronto."

"Hello? That was what I was trying to do." Her nerves were jangling now, mixed with annoyance, because she hadn't done anything to deserve his attitude. "And for the record, I know you require a strict boundary between VaughnTec and your son, and I'm not looking to change that. I don't appreciate you implying otherwise."

"It's your job to follow orders, not dictate their tone.

We might be stuck here together, but that doesn't make us friends."

Sophie drew back, stung. She bit her tongue on the first handful of responses that came to mind, though, because he was partially right. His delivery stank, but she had started to relax her guard around him, and lose sight of the boundaries. It was probably a good thing that he'd reminded her to keep her distance. They were neither friends nor—in the VaughnTec power structure, anyway—equals.

What was more, she absolutely couldn't risk losing this job. For whatever reason Kathleen either hadn't known or had chosen to ignore the rumors that Sophie had been blackballed by one of San Fran's most elite families. Sophie doubted she'd get lucky a second time if she got herself fired from VaughnTec.

So she swallowed the burn of anger, shoved the irrational hurt deep down inside, and nodded. "Fine. We're not friends, and I'm to stay away from Darryn and Luke. Got it. If there's nothing else, I'll go into the other room and send Ava the prints." She could've done it from the kitchen, but she didn't really want to be around him just then.

He nodded, unspeaking, his face a blank mask as she turned, grabbed the fingerprint-covered pages off the table and ran. She didn't care if it looked like retreat or escape, she just wanted to be away from him before she did something stupid. Like cry. Or grab on to him and shake him until the businessman went away and the soldier came back.

GRIFFIN FUMED his way through his first cup of coffee. By the time he started his second cup, he'd leveled off; caffeine had that effect on him, whether he liked to admit it or not. By his third cup, he wanted to kick himself.

Instead, he went in search of Sophie.

She wasn't in the bedroom or sitting room, and the bathroom was empty. He had to assume that even if she was furious with him—which she had every right to be—she wouldn't have left the apartment and gone off on her own. So, hoping to hell she wasn't crying, he knocked on the office door, and then, without waiting for an answer, pushed through.

She was sitting at Erik's desk, staring out the window into the driving snow. She'd pulled the curtains back, but the visibility was so poor it seemed as though there must be another layer of curtains on the other side of the glass, creating a flat white exterior marked with occasional billowing ripples of wind and grayness.

At Griffin's entrance, she turned and looked at him. Her eyes were dry, and filled with a mix of wariness, hurt and anger.

"I'm sorry," he said simply. "I was out of line."

She looked startled for a moment, then her eyes narrowed. "Yes, you were, but I didn't expect you to admit it. Why the change of heart?"

"You want the explanation or the excuse?" Though in reality he wasn't proud of either.

"I want the truth."

"It's a little bit of both. The excuse is that I'm flat-out

inhuman before my first cup of coffee. Ask Darryn. He'll back me up on that."

"I'm not supposed to talk to Darryn," she said sweetly, but with an edge to the words. "So I guess I'll have to take your word on it."

"Which brings me to the explanation." Since she was firmly entrenched behind the big, masculine desk, he moved a pile of landscaping magazines off a nearby chair and sat down. "At the risk of dragging out my apology, I'd like to tell you about Luke's mother."

Sophie shifted, crossing her arms protectively over her chest. "You don't need to. As you correctly pointed out, we're not friends. I'm your executive assistant, nothing more, nothing less."

"I was being an ass. We both know there's more between us than a business relationship, and has been since day one. We've ignored it as best we can, but that doesn't mean it's not there."

She said nothing, simply stared at him with an expression of shock that almost bordered on horror, as though by alluding to their mutual attraction he'd yanked open a big old can of worms. And maybe he had, but after the two sensually charged moments they'd shared the day before, and the fact that it looked like they'd be stranded together another day at a minimum, he had a feeling this was the way to go. Maybe if they talked it out, the tension would disappear. If not, at least the elephant would leave the room.

That was the theory, anyway.

"Be that as it may," Sophie said carefully, avoiding

his eyes as color rode high on her elegant cheekbones. "I thought we agreed not to trade life stories."

"I'd still like you to understand why I'm so protective of my home life." When she didn't say anything, he took it as tacit agreement and continued, "I told you my parents died in a car accident six years ago. I was just back from the marines, had just started getting my feet underneath me at VaughnTec, and then, *wham*. It was just me and Uncle Will left, and, well, suffice it to say neither of us was in a very good place for a long time after it happened." He paused, remembering both the good and the bad. "Ironically, the first couple of buy-ins I made after they died paid off for the company in a big way. Where VaughnTec had barely been making payroll before, suddenly the money started rolling in. Since Will and I were too miserable to do anything but keep working, we plowed every penny back into the company, and it exploded. We were suddenly both very wealthy men."

He broke off, wondering how it could be that such a crazy, awful, wonderful, terrible time in his life could boil down to just a few simple sentences.

"I take it that in this case, wealthy didn't equal happy?"

"Yes and no. Eventually, the shock of it all started wearing off. Will woke up one day, realized he wasn't getting any younger, married the woman he'd been dating on and off for a few years, and asked me to buy him out of the company. I did, of course, but once he was gone, I was damned lonely." He twisted his lips into a completely humorless smile. "I tried to fill the gap with flings and parties, but that wasn't doing it. Then I met Monique." She'd been young, vivacious and pretty. And the way she'd made him feel had reminded him of the way his father had looked at his mother. It'd taken him too long to realize he'd married that memory instead of Monique, who was someone else entirely. "Long story short, we got married too fast, before I figured out that we'd been looking for very different things. I wanted a family like the one I grew up in. She wanted a rich husband."

"The two are not necessarily mutually exclusive," Sophie pointed out.

"They were in this case, except that I didn't have a clue what she was really like, what she was really up to, until I happened to intercept a message from an upscale women's clinic, confirming her appointment for a D & C." He paused, still in disbelief at how close a thing it had been. "I confronted her, and she didn't deny it. Hell, maybe she wanted me to find out, maybe that was how she'd decided to get out of the marriage with a decent enough payoff. Uncle Will had insisted I use a good prenup, so she either had to stay married to me, or she had to come up with some leverage."

"Luke."

"Luke," Griffin confirmed. "I quite literally bought him. In exchange for a hefty payoff, Monique carried the baby to term. She had a C-section as soon as the doctors would let her, had the best plastic surgeon my money could buy give her a nip and a tuck while they had her on the table, and whisked herself away to an exclusive spa to recover from her 'ordeal.'" He paused, and his voice went ragged. "She never even looked at him."

Sophie let the silence linger for a second, broken only by the background howl of the storm winds. Then she said, "No offense, and I don't mean to cross the line—wherever the hell it's been redrawn—but did you ever stop to think that she did you both a favor by being completely out of your lives? Some women shouldn't be mothers, period."

A thread of steel in her expression warned him not to push. Since he was the one who owed the apology, he didn't press, instead saying, "I'm not willing to go so far as to call it a favor, but yeah. I've accepted that Luke and I are significantly better off on our own."

"That wasn't exactly what I said."

"But it's the point I'm trying to make." Griffin leaned forward in his chair, propping his elbows on his knees. "After the initial drama from Monique died down, I started dating again, and I was honest about what I was looking for, someone old-fashioned, who wanted to be a wife to me and a mother to my son. I thought I'd found the right woman about a year ago. Cara was great with Luke, and she said and did all the right things. But when she found out I wanted a prenup, she bailed. She'd been in it for a lucrative lifestyle with the promise of an equally lucrative divorce. She didn't even bother to try pretending otherwise."

"So you've, what? Sworn off dating?" Sophie asked, and he couldn't gauge her thoughts from her voice or expression.

"I've sworn off all of it until Luke's older. When Cara left, he was heartbroken. For a while, any woman he saw, he called her mama, with this hopeful look on his face like he was trying to figure out where she'd gone, or what he'd done wrong. The same thing happened with Kathleen. He's been moping ever since she retired, even though he only saw her now and then. Which is why I don't want you around him. No offense, but we both know that this job is only a waystop for you. You'll be moving on when you're done dealing with whatever you're dealing with. It might be a year from now, it might be three. Who knows? All I know is that I'm not making my son say good-bye again. Not until he understands how life works."

"Or your version of it, anyway," she murmured, and there was a glint in her eyes that he thought might be irritation.

"Look." He spread his hands. "I'm doing the best I know how to do. Luke's doing great with Darryn and me. He doesn't need anyone else. As for me…" He shrugged. "Running VaughnTec and raising my son are my only two priorities right now. I don't have the time or energy for anything or anyone else. Which is why this…this thing between us, this chemistry, or attraction, or whatever, isn't going to go anywhere. But even knowing that, I'm still attracted, which frustrates the hell out of me. And it's largely because I'm frustrated that I snapped at you earlier. I want you, but I don't want to want you, if that makes any sense."

The frustration kicked even higher once he'd said the

words, as though some part of him was hoping she'd throw up her hands, relieved that he'd finally admitted that he wanted her, and jump him.

Instead, she nodded calmly. "Believe it or not, that's exactly how I feel about you. Only I apparently deal with frustration far more politely that you do."

He waited for her to continue. She didn't. "More secrets, Sophie?" he asked quietly when it was clear she didn't intend to elaborate.

She tipped her head. "Not secrets. Privacy."

He wanted to ask more, but knew damn well he didn't have the right. "Fine, then. Privacy." He blew out a breath, discomfited to realize that the tension hadn't faded. If anything, it'd gotten worse.

The need for her churned in his belly, attuning him to her every move, her every breath. The previous night had been torture, with her touching his shoulder, soothing his injuries. He'd been rock-hard, and it'd been all he could manage not to reach for her. And now, it was all he could do not to ask her for a repeat performance, even though his arm felt fine.

"So. What next?" she asked, regarding him steadily, as if in challenge.

We get naked, he wanted to say, but that wouldn't do. So instead, he said, "I'm willing to keep trying the working together thing if you are."

And he was a little surprised to realize it was true. He was honest enough with himself to admit that at least part of his on-again, off-again thoughts of firing Sophie had come from a desire to avoid dealing with his inconvenient attraction to his too-young executive assistant. Having gotten it out in the open might not have mitigated the attraction, but it forced him to acknowledge that it was totally unfair to fire her for being young and pretty, and because he couldn't keep his thoughts where they belonged when it came to her.

That was his problem, not hers.

"I was assuming that much, since you just gave me enough ammunition to make a pretty good case for sexual harassment," she said dryly. "I was actually asking 'what next' in the context of keeping us alive long enough to get back to civilization and a more or less normal working routine."

"Again, that is so not what the women I'm used to dealing with would say under the circumstances," he murmured, continuing to be both baffled and charmed by her, and to a degree that was beginning to worry him.

"And again I'll reply that I'm not those women," she said. "So. What's the plan?"

He wanted to call her on the change of subject, wanted to know what she thought about the two of them, how she was managing to tamp down the attraction. He knew she felt it, too. That wasn't ego talking, it was a fact, gleaned from her nerves and clumsiness, from the faint catch of her breath when they inadvertently touched, and from the almost palpable tension that had hummed in that tiny bathroom, where he'd imagined taking her in his arms and kissing her, putting her up on the edge of the vanity and sliding home.

But he couldn't call her on the subject change any

more than he could follow up on the fantasy. So he answered her question with a question: "What did Ava say about the prints?"

She frowned and shook her head. "I couldn't get through. The signal is seriously weak. Maybe the battery's getting low?"

"Doubtful. If it's powering up, it's got enough juice to send and receive. More likely the storm is messing with the reception."

"Either way, I dropped the files to Martinez's e-mail, which I pulled off the sheriff's department Web site. That way I could turn off the PDA and the pictures should still be in queue."

"Good thinking." Griffin nodded, trying, and mostly succeeding, to make himself focus on their immediate issues rather than the larger complications. She was right, priority number one had to be getting through the rest of the storm, and getting home. Then they would see what might happen between them. Or not. "I think the next step is hitting the woodshed and restocking. I tossed the last log on the fire when I got up, and it's too damn cold to go without."

She nodded and stood. "Then the woodshed it is."

He paused. "Maybe you should stay here. I'm going to go back down into the basement and see if I can find the hidden door. There's got to be one—that's the only explanation for how that lead-fisted bastard got away last night."

"Are you sure I'll be safe here?"

Of course not, and she knew it. He was being selfish,

looking to get some time away from her, to clear his head. But she was right. They were safer together than apart. Period.

He nodded shortly. "Fine. Let's go."

They suited up in silence, but once they were ready to go, he paused by the doorway. "The woodshed isn't far, but it's on a bit of an incline, and I'm betting the drifts are going to be bad. Choose your footing carefully, and if it comes down to a choice, drop the wood rather than hurting yourself, okay?"

She nodded, skin pale in the storm light. "Will do. And Griffin?"

"Yeah."

"Thank you. For telling me about Monique and Luke. I didn't think it would, but it helps to know why you want me to keep my distance from your family."

Too late, Griffin realized he'd let himself get close to her again. They were standing near the door, inside each other's personal space, her face upturned to his in earnest conversation, and all he could think about was how easy it would be to lean down and touch his lips to hers. His blood fired at the thought, his skin tightened and his flesh hardened, making him all too aware that his head might be trying to make the right choice, but his body had other ideas.

Very deliberately, he stepped away from her. He inhaled, trying to settle himself, but that only made it worse because the air carried her soft, feminine scent and the spark of the tension that had existed between them from the first moment, when she'd walked into his office, wide-eyed and nervous, and trying so hard to control her nerves, which had only served to make it worse. His brain had told him to transfer her to another department, but his body must've overruled the logic, because he'd made excuses instead of making the transfer. And now, here they were, closer to each other than his brain liked, not nearly close enough as far as his body was concerned.

Knowing they'd better get moving before he did something to tip the fragile balance, he unbolted the apartment door and yanked it open. "Come on."

At the moment, a short hike through the blizzard was sounding like a very good idea, threat or no threat.

THE STORM WINDS seemed slightly less ferocious to Sophie than they had the day before. Either the blizzard had eased a fraction, or her California-girl self was getting used to bundling up in multiple layers just to venture outside, and spending the rest of the time huddled next to a fireplace.

Or else, she admitted inwardly as she followed the path Griffin was breaking through waist-deep snow, it was easier to think about the weather than it was to think about what had happened back in the apartment. She wasn't sure which information was more staggering in the grand scheme—that he'd bought his son from his gold digging ex-wife and had pretty much sworn off women until Luke was older...or that that she and Griffin had admitted to their mutual attraction.

She probably ought to have felt uncomfortable about

that, but she didn't. She felt empowered. Feminine. And more than a little daring.

Griffin had admitted that he wanted her sexually. He didn't want to want her, granted, but the attraction was there. After what she'd been through with her recently ex-sneak-around-almost-lover, Tony Spellman, and his evil fiancée, Destiny, it was nice to know that a powerful, virile man like Griffin could desire her and be honest about it, without all the subterfuge she'd experienced in that other non-relationship.

Smiling secretly to herself from deep inside the hood of her parka, behind a woolen muffler, she labored through the snow as Griffin reached the woodshed and started kicking snow away from the door, shoving it off to one side. Just as she reached him, he jerked back with a curse.

"Don't look!" He turned and grabbed her and tried to drag her away, but she stayed rooted in place, her eyes locked on to the grisly sight he'd uncovered.

There, leaning up against the woodshed, was a man's body, cold and blue and frozen. He was wearing dark clothes and one glove, with a woolen cap pulled down over his forehead, and a muffler dangling below his chin. His eyes were open and staring, sightless and frozen. Even worse, at least as far as Sophie was concerned, was the patch of red-stained snow near his side, where he'd been gut-shot.

"It's Perry," Griffin said, his voice rough, and sounding too loud in a momentary lull of the storm winds.

"I killed him." At first Sophie didn't know if she'd

said the words or merely thought them, but when she felt Griffin curl his arm around her shoulders despite their earlier conversation about keeping things all business between them, she knew she'd said them aloud. And he wasn't arguing. Worse, he was holding her.

Which meant it was real.

She had killed a man.

Shock rattled through her, freezing her in place. Self-protection or not, the contractor was dead because of her. He had a wife and kids waiting at home for him. Somehow that knowledge made her actions all that much more awful.

"I should have—" She broke off, because what could she say, really? If she hadn't acted, he might have killed her and Griffin. Yet…

"You saved our lives," Griffin said softly, from very close by. Which made her realize that she'd turned toward him, that she was clinging to him, her fingers digging into his parka, her heart drumming in time with the pulse at his throat. In her shock she had reached for him, and he'd let her. More, his arms had come around her and locked on, offering support when she so badly needed it.

Always before, she'd been her own anchor, the one who'd been in charge of things, even when she'd been little more than a child herself.

Now, for just a second, she gave herself permission to cling. She turned her face into Griffin's neck. And wept.

Chapter Seven

Griffin held Sophie, wrapping his arms around her, wishing he could take away what she'd just seen, and the knowledge of what she'd done.

Worse, he wished he didn't notice how right she felt against him. This wasn't the time or place. But he was painfully aware that she was soft and warm and curvy, and fit against him just right, with her head tucked beneath his jaw, her hair brushing against his face and throat. He'd opened his parka so her arms were looped around him beneath the coat, and he'd automatically wrapped the edges of the parka around her, bringing her into his body heat.

He would've liked to get her away from the scene, get her back inside the house, but the trail through the deep snow was too narrow for them to walk together, and he didn't want to let go of her yet.

They stood there, locked together, for a long moment that seemed far simpler than it actually was. The storm lull made for an eerie sort of quiet, an expectant hush.

After a few minutes her sobs passed, and she loosened

her grip on him and pushed away from him. Avoiding his eyes, she said, "I'm sorry." Her voice was low and husky, with a faint tremor of emotion. "That was—"

"Completely understandable," he said, cutting her off. "Come on. Let's get you back to the apartment. I'll take care of the wood."

Inhaling deeply, she scrubbed both hands across her face, leaving her skin rosy pink and her eyelashes heavy with the memory of tears. In that moment, she looked very young and very lost. But then her expression firmed and she shook her head. "No. We're in this together. Tell me what to do."

In reality, the best thing would be for her to go inside and let him have room to do what needed to be done. But the jittering energy that was suddenly pouring off her suggested that she needed to do something active, something more than stand at the window and watch him examine the man she had quite likely killed. So he said, "You're on wood detail. Haul as many loads as you can and stack them just inside the hallway. I'll carry it from there. When you run out of steam on that, maybe you could pull some food together? I don't mean to put you on kitchen detail, but—"

"I don't mind," she said quickly. "Wood. Food. Got it." She moved to pass him, but he caught her arm. Through the layers of clothing and parka, he could feel her trembling.

"Sophie, look at me," he said, and waited until her eyes connected with his. Tension vibrated through her body, and her eyes were dull with shock, yet bright with frenetic energy. He understood both, though wished like hell he could've spared her from it all.

When he didn't say anything right away, she said, "The wind's picking up again. I should get going."

He tightened his grip. "I need you to know that this isn't your fault. You didn't do anything wrong, you hear me? You. Did. Nothing. Wrong."

The tears that had been brimming in her light brown eyes welled up and a single droplet spilled over, tracking down her cheek, which was already wet from the snow and her earlier crying jag. "Please," she whispered. "Just let me go."

Something deep within him said, *I don't want to.* It was that small, seditious voice that had him dropping her arm and taking a big step back, away from her. But he said softly, "We'll talk later."

She nodded, unspeaking, and headed for the woodshed door, deliberately averting her eyes when she passed Perry's corpse.

Griffin watched, wishing to hell he'd left her down in Kenner City the day before. He wasn't sorry he was there—Lonesome Lake was his property, his responsibility. If there was something shady going on there, it was his duty to fix it, especially before he brought Luke out for a visit. But he regretted having involved Sophie, regretted the things she'd been through over the past forty-eight hours, regretted the things she'd been forced to see and do.

"This damn well better be over now that you're dead," he said as he knelt down beside Perry's body.

Problem was, he needed to be sure. Occam's razor suggested that there had been just the single threat, that Perry had gotten into something he hadn't wanted Griffin to know about. But experience, both on the battlefield and in the boardroom, had taught Griffin that human nature didn't necessarily conform to the simplest explanation. Humans were complicated creatures, and because of that, made dangerous enemies. What if Perry wasn't alone?

That was why Griffin decided that his and Sophie's immediate situation trumped police procedure, even though he suspected Martinez and the CSIs would disagree. Still, he was there and they weren't, and he needed to be sure Perry was the man who'd attacked him the day before.

Hunkering down in the stomped-down snow, Griffin examined the body, looking for any evidence that could explain what the contractor had been up to, and whether he'd been working alone or not. A search of Perry's pockets turned up a billfold and some loose change, along with a small, dog-eared spiral-bound notebook containing punch lists, measurements and terse notes about molding and electrical wiring. Which was about what he would've expected from a contractor, and didn't tell him a damn thing about what was going on at Lonesome Lake.

As Griffin searched, he was aware of Sophie passing to and fro, lugging armloads of wood. On her next pass, he called, "That's probably good for now. I'll meet you inside."

She turned back to look at him, her eyes dry, but hollow with shock and grief. "What don't you want me to see?"

"Just go on. Trust me."

She stared at him a moment longer, then nodded. "Okay. But are you certain the apartment is safe?"

They both knew he'd be lying if he said yes. But his gut instinct said they were alone in the mansion now, so he nodded. "You'll be fine. I won't be more than a few minutes behind you."

She nodded and left, though reluctantly.

When she was gone, Griffin focused on the body. The contractor's face was covered with snow and gray with death, but Griffin thought he saw red marks and the beginnings of a bruise along the side of Perry's face, which was consistent with Griffin's adrenaline-jacked memory of struggling with his attacker the day before. Griffin didn't see or feel any evidence of head trauma, and the only blood appeared to have come from the region of the contractor's waist.

Grimacing, Griffin stripped aside Perry's jacket and clothing so he could get a look at the injury. It was a bullet wound, all right, a through-and-through shot at the level of the contractor's right kidney, with the exit wound in the front. It would've been a fatal wound, Griffin knew, as the bullet had most likely taken out the renal artery. There wasn't as much blood as he would've expected, but he had to assume that was a function of the snow having washed it away. Martinez had been lamenting how the blizzard was destroying evidence. Now Griffin could relate.

It had been many years since the last time Griffin had been this up close and personal with death, and never before with the added element of the cold. In a way, the freezing temperatures made it easier, robbing the body of the rubbery, not-quite-warm-enough feeling of the freshly dead. But at the same time the weather complicated things, obscuring any footprints or other evidence, and confusing the blood pattern. He couldn't get past thinking there should've been more blood, but maybe not. It wasn't like he was an expert. The CSIs would be able to get a better idea of what had happened, once the storm broke and they were able to get in and recover the body for processing.

For now, all he could say for certain was that the bullet wound and bruises seemed consistent with what had happened down in the basement the day before.

As he'd been examining Perry, the wind had grown worse and the sky was darkening once again, warning that the lull had only been temporary, and there was more blizzard yet to come. Figuring he'd learned all he was likely to from the body under the circumstances, and also figuring he'd already done enough damage to the scene, he decided he wouldn't compound that by moving the body inside. Instead, he climbed to his feet and slogged back to the house, squinting against a sudden, stinging spray of ice pellets.

Once he was back inside the mansion, he grabbed a huge armload of the wood Sophie had left just inside the door. As he did so, the fine hairs on the back of his neck stayed quiet, and there was an easing of the heavy weight that had been pressing on his lungs ever since he'd realized the bridge collapse had been no accident.

His gut instincts seemed to think Perry had been the sum total of the danger. And he'd never had reason to question his instincts before—at least not on the topic of personal safety. When it came to women, that was an entirely different story. But it was exactly that subject at the forefront of his mind as he headed back to the apartment: women. Or rather, one particular woman.

Sophie had impressed the hell out of him over the past two days. She was gentle, kind and loyal, yet with an unexpectedly fierce fighting spirit, and enough backbone to stand up to him when she deemed it necessary. Yes, she was relatively inexperienced in the business milieu, and far from worldly, but she balanced him in ways he hadn't realized he needed. What was more, there was an aspect of her inexperience that he hadn't even consciously let himself think about before. But now that they had acknowledged the chemistry between them, a small voice deep inside him dared to whisper the words, *Vaughn virgin.*

There was a story on his father's side of the family, a myth, really, passed down from father to son. It said that the Vaughn marriages that worked, the love matches that truly lasted, were to virgin brides.

When Griffin's father had first told him the story, he'd been thirteen and the idea of marrying anyone, virgin or otherwise, had seemed ridiculous. A few years—and a few girlfriends later—he'd all but plugged his ears when his dad brought it up again, because the conversation had involved his mother, and he so hadn't wanted to go there.

The last time they'd talked about it had been a few weeks before the accident. Griffin had been in his early thirties, fresh out of the marines, and ready to take his place within VaughnTec. The idea of settling down and starting a family had been crossing his mind more and more often, at least in an abstract "some day" sort of way, so he'd asked his dad about the legend, and what it meant in real terms.

"I'll keep it general, so I don't skeeve you out again by talking about your mom and me," his old man had said, for which Griffin had been profoundly grateful. "The way I see it," his father had continued, "you'll have to modernize the legend however you see fit. It's not a rule, or even something you should be using as a criterion. But the fact remains that the happiest Vaughn marriages have involved a relatively inexperienced bride. Which isn't to say," his dad had said with a sly grin, "that they don't catch up extremely quickly when they do start gaining some experience."

Which had ended that conversation with Griffin making outraged gagging noises and his father busting a gut. In the aftermath of the accident that'd shifted his world on its axis, Griffin had pretty much walked away from the idea of finding his own Vaughn virgin. Monique hadn't even been close to virginal, but she'd played the role of domesticity so well that he hadn't caught the disconnect until it was too late for their relationship, and almost too late for Luke. Similarly, Cara had proven to him that there was a big difference between ingénue and innocence.

I'm not like those women, Sophie had told him, twice now when he'd compared her responses to those of the other women he'd known. And maybe that was the point.

Which wasn't to say that this the time or place to explore the possibility, Griffin acknowledged inwardly as he thumped a toe against the closed apartment door and called, "Sophie? It's me. Can you get the door?"

But although the circumstances were far from perfect, Griffin thought there was something approaching perfect about the way his heart kicked a little at the sight of her when she opened the door and waved him in, and the way the smell of wood smoke and soup combined to make him feel settled and grounded. Like it or not, he was a traditional man raised by parents who'd held very traditional family roles. Was it any wonder he found himself gravitating toward the same thing in his own life, despite all his intentions to remain apart and alone?

"Thanks." He stacked the wood and fed a couple of logs into the fireplace.

The wind howled outside, and ice pellets dashed themselves against the windowpanes, but for the first time since their arrival, the noise made the apartment seem cozy rather than vulnerable.

"There's soup and baked beans ready to go in the kitchen," Sophie said. "I didn't dish up, because I wasn't sure how long you'd be."

"I'll eat after I've brought in the rest of the wood."

Griffin looked over at her, and saw the remnants of tears on her face, the dull horror still in her eyes. She was being as brave as she knew how, but Perry's death was digging at her. He wished he could tell her she would forget about it in time, that it would matter less because it'd been self-defense, but he couldn't honestly say that. Seven years out of uniform, and he still sometimes saw the faces of the men he'd killed. So instead he said, "Do you want to talk about it?"

She shook her head. "Not really. In fact, I'd really like to turn it all off for a while and take a nap."

He noticed that she'd dragged the mattress back into the bedroom, and returned the sofa cushions to where they belonged. It made sense, given that it appeared as though they had no need to stay away from the windows anymore, and the fire kept all four rooms warm enough. Still, Griffin felt a faint pang, not of disquiet, but of disappointment at the distance it put between them. The message was clear: they would each sleep alone that night.

Which was fine. It was what he wanted, right? It was sure as hell what he'd told her that morning, laying out the bare facts of why there was no future for them, trying his best to convince her when he'd really been trying to convince himself.

She had no way of knowing he'd started to second-guess himself, started to think maybe she was what he'd been looking for—or at least what he should've been looking for—all along. And she didn't need to know it now, either. She was exhausted, physically and emotionally drained. The last thing she needed right now was for him to start changing the rules.

So he waved her to the bedroom. "Go, please. Rest. Recharge. It's been a hell of a couple of days."

She went, but hesitated in the bedroom doorway. "Promise me you won't go out and investigate on your own?"

He wasn't sure if she was afraid of being left alone, afraid he'd get in trouble without her to watch his back, or afraid she'd miss out on part of the impromptu investigation they'd fallen into. Her success at Mickey-Mousing the fingerprints that morning suggested he wasn't the only one who enjoyed the occasional episode of *CSI*. Figuring it covered all three options, he nodded and said, "I'll stay in here until you come back out. I promise."

The rest of the wood could wait, and the thought of the fingerprints had reminded him that he needed to check the PDA and see if he could get through to the sheriff. The sooner he reported Perry's death, the sooner he could see which way Martinez intended to play it, and whether one of the VaughnTec lawyers would need to get involved in order to make sure Sophie didn't suffer any repercussions when the shooting had been pure self-defense.

Sophie nodded, stepped into the bedroom and closed the door softly at her back. But even though she was gone, the cheerful crackle of the fire remained, as did the smell of a hot lunch and the sense that he wasn't alone. Which was something he thought he could get used to. And if a piece of him wondered whether he was getting ahead of himself, creating things that weren't real simply because the two of them were in such an unreal situation, he ignored it as he headed for the kitchen, grabbed a bite to eat, and sat down with Sophie's PDA.

The good news was that the signal strength was decent. The bad news was that the battery side of the equation was less robust, which meant they should start thinking about conserving, in case they were there another day or two.

He found Martinez's number in the PDA's memory, and made the call. The sheriff answered on the third ring, sounding harried. "Martinez here."

"Sheriff, it's Vaughn. How's the weather looking?"

"Another twenty-four hours of heavy snow, minimum. Damn storm system's stalled right on top of us." Martinez paused. "How's it going up there?"

Griffin sketched out the discovery of Perry's body.

When he was done with his report, there was a long silence on the other end of the phone line. Then Martinez sighed. "I'll be honest with you. Part of me hoped it'd go the other way. Not that I'd wish it on anybody to be stranded up there with Vince Del Gardo, but because Perry's one of us. He's a local. And this is going to about kill his wife."

Griffin refrained from pointing out that Perry had very nearly killed both him and Sophie. Instead, he said, "What are the chances he was working with someone up here? Not just on the renovations, but on something he wouldn't want an outsider to see?"

After a moment, the sheriff said, "It's possible, I suppose."

"But you don't think it's likely," Griffin guessed from his tone.

"Honestly? It doesn't play for me. I know you've had troubles with Perry, but before all this happened I would've sworn to you that he's a good man and a good worker. He was the type who hates getting behind schedule, hates not finishing a job to his absolute satisfaction. I would've said that if he told you he was having problems with the reno, then he was having problems, hands down."

Which was consistent with Griffin's initial impression of the man, and why he'd hired him in the first place. But it wasn't consistent with the evidence. "Be that as it may, the bruises and the gunshot wound prove he was the one I fought with down in the basement. And the fact that he attacked us down there seems to make a good argument for him being the one who blew the bridge, too. He didn't want us up here, whatever the reason."

"Goddamned storm," Martinez muttered. "If it weren't for the snow, I'd have the CSU out there. They'd get straight to the bottom of what's going on."

"Did you get Sophie's e-mail?"

"E-mail hasn't exactly been our first priority around here."

"Sophie sent scans of some fingerprints she lifted off the crowbar. Most of 'em are probably mine, but there's at least one thumbprint that isn't. Can you have Ava check them out? She can e-mail Sophie if there's anything else you'd want us to do."

"I think I hear a 'but' in your voice," Martinez said.

"That'd be the part where I'm thinking it's not a priority for her to cross-check the prints. My gut says we're in the clear now that Perry's gone."

"What's your gut's general accuracy rating?"

"Pretty good, except where it comes to women."

"I hear that. Or at least I did until I met my Bree." Martinez paused, and Griffin heard the squawk of a radio in the background. When the sheriff spoke again, he sounded rushed. "Look, I've got to take this. I'll tell Ava to e-mail when she gets the results or if she has any questions. Other than that, you two sit tight for another day or so, okay? We'll get the roads cleared as soon as we can."

The sheriff hung up without waiting for a response, but that was fine with Griffin. He'd done what he'd needed to do, and put the necessary wheels in motion. And, having gotten the sense that Perry was well-liked in the community, and his death would be a shock, Griffin extrapolated that it'd be a good idea to bring in the lawyers sooner than later.

Hitting the batteries for one more quick call, he phoned home and let Darryn know that when the helicopter made it through to pick them up, it should come equipped with a VaughnTec lawyer. After that, Griffin had a quick, garbled conversation with Luke that made him long to be back home with his son. Then, having done what he could do long-distance, Griffin powered down the unit to conserve what was left of the batteries.

He cleaned up his lunch dishes, grabbed a paperback at random from Erik's bookcase, and settled down on the sofa with his feet to the fire. Although part of him was jonesing to get back into the basement and find the hidden passageway that logic said had to be there, he was mindful of his promise to Sophie. She'd needed to know that he was going to be there when she woke up, so that was exactly what he intended to do.

And, thinking that, he dozed off with the book on his chest, alert to sounds or alarms, but otherwise letting himself drift, and think of what might be. Those thoughts kept circling back to Sophie. And instead of pushing them away, as he would've done before, he went with the flow, into a world of warmth, soft sighs, and innocence.

He awakened some time later, jolted back to full consciousness by a hint of sound, a furtive movement. The light was dimming toward the quick winter dusk, darkening the already low illumination afforded by the storm skies. But the cool blue light was sufficient to show him Sophie, standing in the bedroom doorway. She was wearing a too-large T-shirt that covered her nearly to her knees, with jeans below, as though she'd slept in the T-shirt and pulled on the jeans before coming out of the bedroom. Her hair was loose, tumbling to her shoulders and her expression was wary.

Griffin was on his feet and across the room before he was aware of moving. He stopped near her and looked past her into the bedroom, but saw nothing amiss. "What's wrong?"

"I've been thinking."

He winced. "About Perry. Look, I know it'll probably

be a while before you're ready to believe it, but you didn't have a choice. It was him or us. I see it that way, and the law's going to see it that way." If not, the VaughnTec lawyer would make sure of it.

Her eyes went hollow at the mention, but she shook her head. "I wasn't thinking about what happened to Perry. Or at least not directly. I was thinking about everything you said this morning, about how we should just keep working together and ignore the attraction."

"About that," he began. "I've been thinking—"

She lifted her hand and touched her fingertips to his lips, silencing him. "Don't. Please. Not until I've finished saying what I want to say to you. It took me nearly an hour to gather the courage to come out here. If I derail now, we might not get another chance at this."

Griffin's blood thrummed in his veins as he got an inkling of where her thoughts had taken her. And although he liked to think he wouldn't have even considered it, would've stopped her there, if he hadn't been doing some major rethinking of his own, the reality was that he couldn't be sure. He wanted her that much. But because he *had* been rethinking things, when she took her hand away from his mouth, he nodded encouragement. "Go on. I won't interrupt."

The hollow look drained from her eyes, to be replaced with a spark, one he suspected was a reflection of the heat that had roared to sudden life inside him. Her lips curved as she said, "Something tells me you're catching up."

"The sheriff says it'll be at least another twenty-four hours before the storm lets up."

"Then that's twenty-four hours that we can both agree will cease to exist once the storm breaks and we get back to reality." She paused, then said softly, "I can't help thinking that it could've so easily been you or me, or both of us, out there leaning up against the woodshed, dead and gone. And I decided that life's too short, and I've spent too much of it already doing the things I ought to do, or that I have to do. I want to take something for myself. I want to take *this* for myself, even if it's nothing but a memory by the time the storm breaks."

Griffin knew he should say something, to tell her that he'd been an idiot that morning, and that he hoped whatever they were about to start could last beyond their time together at Lonesome Lake. But his voice had stopped working, and his brain could form only one coherent thought as he stood there, looking down at her and seeing the faint hint of wariness along with a spark of challenge in her light brown eyes.

That thought was: *I want.* There was no other rationality than that. Nothing mattered beyond it.

And because he had no voice, and no thoughts other than of her, and because he, at least, knew there might be more than a single night for them, he did what he'd wanted to do from the very beginning.

He leaned in. And touched his lips to hers.

The first moment of the kiss was a shimmer of warmth, the second a bite of electricity, just as Sophie herself was soft innocence covering an edge of excitement. She parted her lips on an exhalation of surprise and pleasure, or maybe the surprise and pleasure were his, he didn't know anymore where his desire left off and hers began.

He crowded closer and deepened the kiss, slanting his mouth across hers and delving with his lips and tongue, suctioning gently, asking for access.

If he'd expected to have to cajole a response, he was way off base. She met him head-on, headlong, opening to him on a murmur of pleasure and leaning into the kiss. She slid her tongue along his, shaping his lips with hers and bringing a sharp wash of sensation he hadn't expected, wasn't prepared for.

They touched at only two points—where she held his hand against her cheek and where their lips met in ever-increasing fervency—but raw need roared through him as though they were twined together, horizontal, tearing at each other's clothes.

Heat flared and his blood pounded in his veins, tensing him, hardening him, bringing him close to the point of madness. He wanted her naked, wanted her pressed against him, underneath him, above him, hell, pinned against the wall; he'd take her any way he could get her, any way that was humanly possible.

The compulsion hammered through him, driven higher when she curled her fingers around his hand, anchoring them together. He lifted his free hand, needing to touch her, to undress her.

That was when she stepped back and smiled at him. And led him into the bedroom.

Chapter Eight

When Sophie's mother had spoken to her about sex, she'd talked about power and the things a woman could make a man do for her in exchange. Sophie's high-school girlfriends used sex to be popular, or rebellious, or whatever. And when she'd finally gotten out from underneath the burden of being her mother's primary caregiver and the sole supporter of their two-person family unit, she'd focused on her studies, then her new job. Tony had been an aberration, and though he'd seemed sincere, she learned soon enough that to him, sex was a game. Never once, really, had she understood sex as it was touted in the media, as a transcendental experience. Nor had she had sex with Tony, or anyone before him, simply because it hadn't felt right.

Until now.

She led Griffin into the bedroom, which was dark with the dusk and the storm, illuminated only by the single candle she'd lit when she'd awoken from her nap with two thoughts pounding in her head, in her veins: Griffin wanted her, and she wanted him.

She'd thought it through, and had tried to argue herself out of the decision, only to come back to the basic reality that there wouldn't be another night like this, a night out of their normal realm. Danger had brought them together, and violence had made her step back and look at what might've happened, what experiences she might've died without.

It was time. It was right. With him.

When they reached the side of the bed, she slid open the bedside table to reveal the box of condoms she'd found there. They were obviously a joke gift to Erik; each packet had some version of a saying about the wearer being over the hill. If she'd believed in karma she might've taken the presence of condoms in a retired couple's bedside table as a cosmic sign that she was making the right decision. As it was, she'd simply been grateful for the find.

Griffin's lips twitched, and his dark green eyes sparked with self-deprecating humor. "I'll do my best to prove that the sayings don't apply."

"They haven't hit their expiration date," she said, speaking of the condoms, because their ability to do their job was really all she cared about. Not only because the last thing she needed was another complication in her life, but also because of what Griffin had told her about his past experiences, and the women who had tried to manipulate him. The last thing she wanted would be for him to ever put her in that category.

He grinned. "Hopefully, I haven't hit my expiration date, either."

That had her tipping her head to one side. "The age gap bothers you?"

His grin faded as he shook his head. "No. Trust me, it doesn't. I'll tell you why later. Right now I have other things on my mind."

Then, though she'd been the one to offer the invitation and lead him into the bedroom, he took charge. Not by making a forceful move, or by dominating her physically, but by simply being there. With her. Because she'd asked.

"Sophie," he said, just her name, and leaned in and touched his lips to hers.

The heat came instantly, springing from the well of desire she'd kept tucked away where she'd thought he couldn't see it, and gaining an edge of desperation from their recent brush with death.

He changed the angle of the kiss, slanting his mouth across hers and requesting access, demanding it. She softened on a sigh of rightness, a click of connection, and his tongue swept inside to touch hers. In that moment, rationality disappeared, and reality ceased to exist.

Her blood roared in her veins, skimming through her body and tingling at the points where he touched her, lifting his hands to skim up her arms, brush along her temple and jaw, and then finally settle around her, encompassing her and urging her into the warmth and strength of his big body.

She stepped into him, fitted herself against him, and nearly reeled at the added sensations: her breasts pressing up against the wall of his chest; the hard ridge of his erection settling against her; and the continued magic of his hands playing over her, shaping her, caressing her through the thin nightshirt, then beneath it to her skin.

"Touch me," he groaned, his tone caught somewhere between a plea and a demand, and she complied gladly, sliding her arms around his waist, then beneath his shirt where it had come free as he'd slept.

Running her hands up the strong columns of muscle on either side of his spine, she pressed into him as she'd imagined doing the day before, when he'd been bare to the waist and she'd wanted to put her hands on him, her lips.

As though he'd read her mind, he pulled away and yanked his shirt and sweater off over his head with a powerful, impatient move. That impatience was echoed in his intense, focused expression as he reached for her once again, kissed her once again, and his intensity brought an echoing spear of desire stabbing within her.

"Come here," he said softly, and drew her down to the unmade bed, where she'd woken an hour ago, thinking of him. Wishing they could be together despite their differences.

Now, as she followed him down and lay beside him, touching him, kissing him, there was no gap between them in age or station—she was woman to his man, softness to his strength. There was a definite gap in experience, but he seemed to instinctively understand that, though maybe not the degree. Regardless, when she paused or fumbled, unsure of where her hands belonged, or whether she was doing things right, he smoothed over the moments by guiding her, or simply by holding still and letting her find her way.

She touched his chest, following the hard ridges of muscle and delighting in the contrast of smooth, warm skin and wiry, masculine hair. He lay back, fisting his hands in the bedclothes as she moved to trace the same paths with her lips, learning the taste of him, the feel of him.

His harsh breathing quickened. She could feel the tension vibrating through his big frame, and knew he was giving her this time, giving her himself, because he knew she needed it. And with each touch and kiss her nerves smoothed and the heat coiled higher within her. She grew brazen, brave, and when lips and hands weren't enough anymore, she sat up away from him and drew her shirt off over her head.

He just lay back, anchored by the grip of his hands in the sheets. And looked at her in the candlelight.

She saw the approval in his eyes and reveled in it. Chills chased across her bare skin and tightened her nipples when he whispered, "You're beautiful, Sophie."

Other men had complimented her looks before. But he was the first to really know her before he complimented her, to really see *her* as he was saying the words. So instead of blushing or covering up, as she might have done otherwise, she stayed there, rocked back on her heels on the mattress above him, and let him look his fill. And when he released his anchoring hold and reached up to trace a fingertip along the edge of one of her breasts, she shivered against the heat and sensation brought by the caress, but didn't move. She stayed still, letting him learn her body as she had begun to learn his.

He drew her down and touched his lips to her mouth, her cheeks, and the sides of her throat. And all the while, he caressed her, skimming his hands along her ribs and waist, across the sensitized skin of her stomach and up to cup her breasts and then away again, each time making her hotter, bringing her higher.

Desire raged in her, and impatience took root. Soft, gentle kisses and touches ceased to be enough. She wanted more.

Emboldened now, no longer fumbling or frantic, she guided his hands to the button of her borrowed jeans, and helped him strip the last of her clothing away. He unhooked his belt and skimmed out of his jeans, as well, then lay back down beside her, so they were just barely touching. She reveled in the heat pouring off his slick skin, the quick tap of the pulse at his throat, and the absolute focus in his eyes, which let her know he was entirely in the moment, there with her.

Crowding closer to him, so they touched and twined together from nose to toes, she pressed her lips to his, opened her mouth beneath his, and poured herself into the kiss. Another time, if there was another time for them, she would touch and taste him again, learning the lower half of his body as she had learned his upper half. But now, this time, she was ready for more. Beyond ready. She was burning, pulsing with desire and caught in a building wave of intensity that fired her heart to a frenzied cadence.

Make love with me, she wanted to say, but didn't because she knew what they were doing wasn't love, not really, and didn't want to dress it up as such. Yet she couldn't bring herself to offer a coarser version of the invitation, either, because she had to believe this was more than the sex her mother had used as power, the "getting it on" the girls had giggled over in high school, or the mean, hurtful thing Tony had twisted it into.

So in the end she said nothing. Or rather, she let her body speak for her. *I want this,* her lips said to him, *I want you*.

He shifted against her, sliding his hand down to grip her hip, her upper thigh, and then her knee. He guided her leg up and over him, so her calf was hooked around him and she was open to his soft, whispering caresses.

She arched against him, opened to him and let herself ride the rising tide of sensation. He kissed her, whispered hot promises, praise and the things he wanted to do with her. Restless now, she reached for him, taking hold of his erection and reveling in the feel of soft, velvety skin over hot, hard flesh.

A groan ripped through him and his body tensed to rigor for a second, then eased, letting her know just how hard he was fighting to go slowly, to make it last. To make it matter.

Warmth rolled through her, sweeter than the heat, though no less powerful. She opened her eyes—when had they drifted closed?—and found his face very near hers, his expression intent. When their gazes met she felt a new flare of heat, an added click of connection that let her know that this was good and right for her, that it was what she wanted and needed.

"Are you sure?" he asked in a whisper, offering her a last out.

But there was no turning back for her, hadn't been since the moment she'd finally risen from the bed and gone out into the main room to take what she wanted. He was what she wanted, in that moment, all other considerations aside.

She let him see the heat in her eyes, the need and the confidence he'd given her, and that she'd taken for herself. "I'm very sure."

He smiled, and it seemed to her that the warmth in his eyes was more than desire when he said, "I'm glad."

He reached past her, covering her with his body for a moment as he retrieved one of the condoms. He ripped through the silly slogan, pulled out the latex sheath and covered himself in a practiced move that was somehow more elegant than she had imagined it being. Then he was rising over her again, settling himself between her legs and pausing, as if to give her a chance to get used to his weight. But she was done with pausing, done with taking it slow. She reached up and kissed him, openmouthed and inciting, a wordless demand for completion.

Take me, the **kiss** said. And he did.

He surged against her, into her, breaching the slight resistance of her virginity in a pinch of pain that was quickly lost to the strangeness of having a piece of him inside her, filling and stretching her.

"You okay?" he asked, his voice rough with tension, and maybe something else.

She looked into his eyes, looking for surprise or accusation and finding something much more complicated, more compelling. In answer, she kissed him and hooked a leg around his, urging him to move.

And, on a long, shuddering exhale, he did. She could almost see the restraint fall away from him, could feel it in the surge of his body as he withdrew from her and thrust home, and in the fervor of his kiss.

The sensation of his penetration went from strangeness to pleasure, then kindled to a flame. She moved against him, matching his thrusts and then demanding more as the tempo increased and the power of the act coiled tightly inside her. She grabbed on to him, dug into him, and in answer he hooked an arm at her knee and raised one of her legs, spreading her, baring her to the slide of his body against hers.

She cried out at the sensations that brought, and again when her body somehow clamped onto him, tightening around the point of their joining. He spoke to her, urging her on, telling her to trust him, to trust them. She heard his voice but didn't process the words; her entire being was focused on the pleasurable tightness inside, and the sense that there was something bearing down on her, something huge and important.

They surged together and apart, together and apart, and she clung to him, giving herself over to the feelings they made together, until finally she reached that huge place inside her, or it reached her, she wasn't sure which, or even where she was, or who. Pleasure coalesced into a hard knot at the point where she and Griffin connected, growing tighter with each thrust until the balance tipped and the hard knot went nova, bursting into a brilliance of heat and sensation that had her bowing back on the bed, her mouth open in a silent scream.

Griffin moved urgently against her, drawing out the moment. Then, just as she was coming down from the peak, he picked up the tempo once again, thrusting surely and rhythmically, his hot cheek pressed against hers. A hollow groan built in his chest and became her name, and then he was shaking and driving into her, shouting as he found his own release. His excitement put her over again and she came a second time, shuddering in his arms and holding on to him, using his solid strength as her anchor.

The pleasure drained then, going from urgency to a background hum of completion. They were both breathing hard, and Sophie was aware of fine tremors running through her body, little post-coital bursts of satisfaction.

Griffin whispered something—praise, perhaps, or maybe simply her name—and rolled off her to one side. He gathered her against him, fitting her close as her breathing slowed and her skin cooled.

"Cold?" he murmured, and drew a blanket up over them before she could answer, once again seeming to know what she needed before she did.

Sophie had never felt so in tune with another human being. Or, for that matter, with herself. She knew reality would intrude soon enough. The storm winds were still blowing outside, lashing icy snow against the window-panes in a dusk that had gone to night. But the weather would break eventually, and they would have to deal with Perry's death, and saying good-bye to what they'd found together at Lonesome Lake, both the good and the bad. For now, though, she was determined to stay in the moment, with the man she'd claimed for herself, if only for a short time.

Cuddling into him, she threaded her fingers with his, turned her face into his throat, and let herself drift. She should probably say something, she knew. And she'd get around to it, in a moment. For right now, all she wanted to do was lie there with him, feeling deliciously and thoroughly taken, and pretend for a few seconds that the rightness she was feeling could last forever.

GRIFFIN LAY AWAKE a long time after Sophie drifted off to sleep. He listened to the storm winds and the beat of his own heart, and waited for guilt to descend, along with its close cousins, regret and panic.

Except they didn't come.

The lessons hard learned in his past suggested that it would be a mistake for him to get involved with a woman, any woman, even one as genuine as Sophie. But at the same time, he couldn't ignore the inner resistance of her maidenhood, sure evidence that she'd come to him a virgin.

The responsibility of that, expressed or implied, should've had him up and out of the bed, and halfway down the mountain, blizzard or not. Instead, he stayed cuddled up against her, idly wondering which he should do first, scrounge for food or wake her up and see if he could ease her into round two.

As he did so, two words worked their way inside his skull, in a voice that sounded like his father's. *Vaughn virgin*. And again, something that probably should have freaked him out, failed to do so.

She was what he'd been looking for, he realized on a burst of wonder, along with something that might quickly become love. He'd wanted his match, his Vaughn virgin, and hadn't even known it.

Satisfaction expanded within him, stretching his chest and putting a wide smile on his face. Feeling primed and ready for more, yet conscious that she might not be, he eased away from her and crawled from the bed. He cleaned up and disposed of the condom, thinking with an inner smirk, *So much for those over-the-hill slogans*.

Pulling on his jeans and taking the candle for light, he headed to the kitchen and did what he could to assemble a snack from the canned provisions in Gemma's pantry. When he returned, Sophie stirred and woke, blinking in the candlelight.

He stopped in the doorway, feeling his heart give an uncharacteristic thump in his chest as he searched her face for evidence of regret. "Hey."

She smiled, her expression one of hesitant pride. "Hey, yourself."

And somehow, that was all that needed to be said. He crossed the room and set the snacks within reach, though he suspected it would be some time before they got around to eating. Then he slid back beneath the covers. And into her arms.

They ate eventually, slept little and talked even less. The entire night was given over to their bodies, and the pleasure they found together, which filled a hollow inside him that he hadn't even acknowledged before.

When dawn broke and still the storm raged on, he found a piece of himself wishing it would never end. But at the same time, he wanted to get back to civilization, and deal with the inevitable fallout from what had happened to him and Sophie at Lonesome Lake. They would need to do that before moving forward.

For a while the day before, he'd been thinking he would resell the estate, that he'd never want to return, and certainly not with Luke. Now, though, he was starting to reconsider. Something terrible had happened to him there, it was true. But something wonderful had happened, too.

Touching his lips to Sophie's temple, he eased from the warm bed into the chilly winter air of the apartment. *The fire must've died*, he thought. And no wonder, because he'd had things on his mind other than keeping the fireplace going.

Whistling softly so as not to wake Sophie, who was deeply asleep, he got dressed and tiptoed out to the main room to resuscitate the fire. As it slowly came back to life, he headed to the kitchen for his first cup of coffee, figuring he'd save Sophie from his early morning ogre routine, though he was feeling damned civilized, considering the lack of caffeine.

Maybe that was what love did to a guy, he thought.

Then he stopped dead, and waited again for the panic, and the knee-jerk "no way in hell, not me" reaction. Only it didn't come.

And okay, maybe two days stranded together in a blizzard, and one night spent together, was too short a time to fall in love, but what about the month prior to that, when they'd been circling around the attraction, and learning each other's rhythms and quirks? Maybe, for him and Sophie, at least, that had been a sort of courtship.

Trying on the idea of love and a future, and finding that it fit far better than he would've expected, he snagged her PDA off the counter and powered it up. He wanted to check in with Martinez and see how much longer they'd be stranded up at the estate, and whether the lawyers needed to be doing anything in the interim.

The coffeemaker started bubbling as the PDA came online, showing that there was no current phone or Internet signal, but there were two e-mails in Sophie's inbox.

Figuring they were from Ava Wright, confirming that the fingerprints Sophie had lifted from the crowbar came from Perry Long—or at least didn't match Vince Del Gardo—he clicked over to the e-mail and opened the first message.

He skimmed a few lines, and froze.

Dear Sophie, However did you manage to hook yourself up with Griffin Vaughn? Does he know what kind of a schemer you are, how you tried to black-mail your last boss and nearly got away with it? Does he know that you're maxed out on three different credit cards, in default on your student loans and looking for an easy way out? I suspect not. Quit now, leave town, and he'll never have to find out. If you stay, I'll make sure he knows everything. I won't let you do to him what you tried to do to me.

The message was unsigned, the address a generic jumble of initials and numbers, hosted by one of San Fran's major providers.

Griffin just stood there, stunned, coffee forgotten as the morning's foolish joy curdled to anger.

Sophie might've been a different sort of woman from the others, but she'd played the same game. And he'd damn well nearly fallen for it again.

SOPHIE AWOKE sore and satisfied, without a hint of regret or remorse. There were some nerves, though, mainly at the thought that she and Griffin could very well make it down off the mountain by nightfall, and she'd have to deal with what came next.

Though a foolish part of her wanted to believe that Griffin's tenderness the night before had been affection, that his whispered promises of a future had been real, she knew those wishes belonged locked up with her dreams of a law degree and a chance to fight for the rights she and her mother had been denied. Her wistful fantasies of a future with Griffin were just as lovely, and just as unlikely. She had to at least try to be realistic.

Still, she couldn't help feeling a bubble of optimism

as she raided Gemma's closet and dresser for another shirt and a clean pair of jeans. She felt different. Hell, she *was* different.

Granted, there was a darkness in her heart that came from having found Perry's body the day before. She was grateful that she and Griffin were safe, but wished that could've come at a price other than a man's life, even a man who had attacked them, and probably would have killed them if she hadn't pulled the trigger. Self-defense or not, she knew she would carry the weight of his death for a long time to come. But somehow that didn't overshadow the specialness of what she and Griffin had found together. The two very different emotions existed side-by-side. Or maybe the joy she'd found in her own body was helping her deal with the guilt and sorrow. She didn't know.

What she did know, however, was that she was starving. She could smell coffee, and even that was enough to get her stomach rumbling. Grinning at the thought of what she'd done to work up that appetite, she headed for the kitchen, trying not to feel strange about seeing Griffin in the light of day, after the things they had done to each other in the darkness.

The snappy greeting she worked up died the moment she stepped into the kitchen and got a look at his dark, brooding countenance.

She crossed the room, reaching for him, but something in his eyes had her stopping a few feet away, her hands dropping to her sides as her stomach did barrel rolls and hunger turned to nerves. "What's wrong?"

He didn't answer right away, just sat there at the kitchen table, staring at her. Her PDA lay on the table beside his hand, next to an empty coffee cup. The presence of the handheld computer suggested that he'd gotten terrible news. But what was it? Possibilities cascaded through her mind, all having to do with the estate and the police, and the body that sat where it had fallen, out in the snow. Her heart shuddered in her chest. "Is Martinez going to press charges?"

The sheriff had to follow protocol, she supposed, and in a fair world she wouldn't have anything to worry about. Unfortunately, her own experiences had taught her that life was far from fair. Worse, a few minutes earlier, she would've said that Griffin would be on her side if it came to a court battle. But now, looking into his eyes and seeing nothing of the man who'd made love to her the night before, she wasn't so sure.

Her voice dropped to a whisper as she forced the words through a suddenly closed throat. "Griffin, say something. You're scaring me."

"When were you going to tell me about your debts?" His voice was flat and rough. Accusatory.

The question was so far from anything she might've expected him to say, that it took her brain a moment to catch up and process the words. And even then, all she could do was stare at him in shock. "Excuse me?"

He spun the PDA to face her. It was down to its last bar of battery power, but that wasn't what caught her attention. No, it was the e-mail address that had her heart clogging her throat and a kick of desperate tears filming her eyes.

The address belonged to Destiny Marlowe. Or rather, she supposed the name was Destiny Spellman now, because she and Tony had married recently, hadn't they?

It had been Destiny who'd tracked Sophie down based on an errant phone message, Destiny who'd revealed that Sophie and Tony's almost-affair had been nothing more than his pre-wedding jitters, a last fling that the powerful up-and-coming lawyer had turned into a game. It had been Destiny who hadn't been satisfied with Sophie breaking off the relationship, Destiny who had been determined to drive her out of San Francisco altogether, not understanding that it wasn't an option for Sophie to leave town, not with her mother finally installed in a state-subsidized longterm care facility.

Sophie had hoped Tony's vengeful bride would be satisfied at having used her high-placed family's considerable connections to have Sophie blackballed, not only at the employment office of the business school where she'd graduated at the top of her class, but also at just about every major company in the metro region except for VaughnTec.

And now she'd ruined even that. Sophie could see it in Griffin's eyes.

She scanned the message, though she could've guessed what it contained—the same blend of half-truths and evidence Destiny had used elsewhere. The words almost didn't matter. What mattered was that Griffin had undoubtedly checked and learned that yes, indeed, Sophie was way over her head in debt, with little hope of digging her way out on her present salary.

And because of what Monique and Cara had done to him before, and the way his mind worked, he'd convicted her without the benefit of a trial, or even an opportunity to speak on her own behalf.

Anger and disappointment rolled through her, along with the crushing weight of grief. "So this is how it's going to be?" she asked softly, hoping against hope that he'd soften, even slightly, and ask for her side of the story.

"No," he countered, "I'm about to tell you how it's going to be. When we get out of here, I'm terminating your employment at VaughnTec. My lawyers will help you deal with any fallout from Perry's death, because the fact remains that you saved our lives by shooting him. But that's where my responsibility ends, understand? I'm not paying you a damned dollar beyond your salary, and I had better not hear the first hint of any sort of sexual harassment talk. You try that garbage on me and you'll be seriously sorry."

Sophie wanted to crumble beneath his words as he piled rage atop anger atop accusations she could only defend if he chose to believe in her.

Tears filled her eyes and spilled over, tracking down her cheeks, born from both sorrow and anger. A few months earlier, in the aftermath of what had happened with Tony, she'd thought she'd hit the lowest point in her life. Clearly she'd been wrong, because the pain that echoed in her chest now was ten times worse than what she'd felt when Destiny had shown up at her workplace, told her about Tony's perfidy and gotten her fired, all within the space of twenty minutes.

The emotions she'd felt back then had been a mix of hurt and shame. The grief that slammed into her now, threatening to drive her to her knees, was made of both those things, along with a keening sense of loss and betrayal.

Struggling not to sag beneath that burden, she lifted her chin and used her sleeve to wipe the streaming tears away. "Please give me a chance to explain."

"Explain what? I checked the facts. Evidence doesn't lie."

She sniffed back a fresh bout of tears, seeing from the cold rage in his eyes and the uncompromising set to his jaw that there would be no use talking to him now. His mind was made up, not just by the anonymous e-mail he'd happened to stumble across—which must have recalled how he'd learned of Monique's planned abortion—but also because he'd confirmed the so-called evidence.

She could've told him that he was no CSI, that even hard evidence could be interpreted in different ways, but what would be the use? He'd gotten where he was in life by being stubborn and hard-nosed, and wasn't likely to change.

Bowing her head in a vain attempt to keep him from seeing how upset she was, she whispered, "Fine. No harassment charges." She never would've gone after him for harassment, especially given that she'd arguably been the aggressor the night before. Heck, she'd never seriously considered going after Tony for harassment. Not that Griffin would believe her if she told him that, though. He'd made up his mind.

Suddenly unable to stay in the apartment a moment longer, she spun and fled the kitchen. She didn't stop to think or plan; she just stuffed her feet in the boots she'd been using, and grabbed Gemma's parka off the rack.

She had her hand on the apartment door when Griffin said from behind her, "Where do you think you're going?"

"Out." She unlocked the deadbolt and yanked the door open.

"That might not be such a good idea."

"Oh?" She spun on him, letting loose some of the fury she was trying to keep inside, knowing that if she set the anger free, the rest of the emotions she was fighting so hard to keep in check would soon follow. Advancing on him, hands fisted at her sides, she grated, "And what would you prefer I do? Stay in here with you?" When she saw the answer in his eyes, she shook her head. "I didn't think so."

"Don't leave the mansion," he said. "I don't want you freezing to death on my watch."

With the implication that she was welcome to do exactly that once they were away from Lonesome Lake.

"I can take care of myself." God knew she'd been doing it since she was thirteen.

Knowing if she stayed a moment longer she would lose it completely, she turned her back on him and stepped out into the hallway. It was empty, of course, but it didn't feel lonely until she heard the apartment door close, and heard the deadbolt click into place.

For the first time since their arrival, she was alone outside the relative safety of the apartment perimeter.

But Perry was dead. And, as she'd said to Griffin, she could take care of herself. Realistically, all she had to do was find someplace to wait out the last bit of the storm. Once she'd picked a likely spot to hunker down, she'd return to the apartment for some supplies—food, some pillows, maybe a chair and one of Erik's books. A lantern. The basics.

Feeling a little more settled having a plan of sorts, she headed down the hallway and across the mansion, toward the far wing, where she remembered seeing some rooms with actual walls and flooring, and one even with sunny yellow paint on the walls.

She figured she could use a little sunshine right about then.

When she came to the door leading to the basement, she couldn't help looking at it, shuddering and hurrying past. She was halfway down the corridor leading to the yellow room when she heard a board creak behind her.

She spun with a gasp, but it was already too late.

Something slammed into the side of her head, and darkness rose up to claim her.

Chapter Nine

Griffin knew he'd done the right thing. He'd called to check out the e-mailer's story before confronting Sophie, hoping against hope that it'd turn out to be baloney, or something that could be easily explained, but had gotten blown out of proportion in the anonymous e-mailer's mind.

But he'd had no such luck. He'd burned through almost all of the PDA's remaining battery power making the calls, only to learn that Sophie owed nearly fifty thousand dollars split among three credit cards, on which she'd been paying no more than the minimum. She'd taken out student loans for her business courses— not just for tuition, but for living expenses, as well. Those loans were several months in arrears, and headed for collections.

Despite her apparent lack of financial smarts, however, she'd aced her classes, graduated and had taken a job at the prestigious law firm of Wade & Kane, where she must've met—and apparently come close to seducing—her boss. Not that Griffin had been able to get that information prior to business hours, but given that the other facts matched with the e-mail, he'd been forced to assume that one did, too.

Besides, she hadn't denied it.

"Goddamn it." Griffin scrubbed a hand across his chest, which hurt with a steady, insistent ache he wanted to say was a pulled muscle, but suspected was his heart.

He was on his third cup of coffee, but neither the anger nor the hurt had faded with the influx of caffeine. If anything, the ache had gotten worse.

Scowling, he punched in a familiar number, figuring he could bark at Kathleen's voice-mail, if nothing else.

To his surprise, she answered on the second ring. "Hello? Sophie?"

Something dark and nasty twisted in his gut. "It's Griffin."

There was dead silence, then a quiet, "Oh. Hell."

Since he didn't remember ever hearing his former assistant curse, that was another surprise, but the effect was lost to a roaring sense of betrayal. He'd thought Kathleen's lack of response to his occasional voice-mails meant she'd left her PDA behind as part of retiring, or maybe that she never checked her messages. Not that she'd been screening.

Of all the women in his life, she'd been the one he'd trusted. And even she, it seemed, had a hidden agenda. Anger spiking hot and ugly, he growled, "So you're taking her calls and not mine, is that it? Any particular reason for that?"

"Actually, Sophie's never called me, though I encouraged her to do so if she had any trouble with you," Kathleen said in the level, faintly chiding voice she'd perfected over her nearly six years of working for him. "So I figured if she was calling me now, it was important."

"And my calls weren't important?"

"You needed a clean break so you'd give her a chance." Kathleen paused. "Since you're calling from a work number that's popping up her name on the caller ID, can I assume that you at least haven't fired her yet?"

That hit close to home, roughening Griffin's voice when he said, "Please tell me you didn't know about what happened at her last job."

"Tony Spellman? I knew about him."

Disbelief heightened his outrage. "And her debts?"

"I figured between the blackballing and the money she owes, she'd be likely to stick with you long after most of my other choices would've quit. It's not like you're an easy guy to work for, you know."

She'd told him that time and again over the years, with varying degrees of amusement. But there was zero humor in it for him. Not now. "Why her, Kath? There had to be a dozen older, better qualified applicants for the position. I may be a pain in the ass, but I pay well."

There was such a long pause he thought she wasn't going to answer. Then she sighed and said, "There's something about her, isn't there, Griffin? She has this quality that makes you feel as though she's completely in the moment, experiencing life as though everything is fresh and new. I wanted that for you, Griffin. I wanted it for you and Luke."

Suddenly the storm wasn't raging outside anymore. It was inside him, tearing at his chest. "You were *matchmaking*?"

"Don't sound so horrified. It wasn't like you were going to meet the woman of your dreams at one of those chi-chi charity balls. You tried that. It didn't work. So I found you a good girl. If you didn't notice her, so be it." Her voice went sly. "I'm guessing you noticed her."

"Actually, my complete lack of response is over you calling her a 'good girl.' For crap's sake, she's up to her neck in debt, and she seduced her last boss!" Or had tried to, anyway. He knew firsthand that it hadn't gone all the way. Which was something he was trying very hard not to think about just then.

"The seduction was the other way around, despite rumors to the contrary," Kathleen corrected. "Which, by the way, were started by his ticked-off bride-to-be. As for the debts, the vast majority of them are from her mother's medical issues, which Sophie has been dealing with since she was thirteen." A pause. "Is it worth me pointing out that you should've asked her this yourself rather than calling me?"

"I—" Griffin began, and then broke off, partly because he had absolutely no defense, and partly because the PDA had started emitting the rhythmical beeping noise that indicated he had three minutes left on his battery. "Long story. Look, I'm losing my battery, and I have one more call to make."

He was about to hang up when Kathleen said, "Griffin, wait. I want you to do me a favor."

"What?"

"Give her a chance. Whatever is or isn't happening between you two, give it a chance, okay? That sweet boy of yours needs a woman's touch, and so do you."

He hung up without answering, because what could he say? He couldn't believe that Kathleen had picked Sophie, not as his executive assistant per se, but as someone he might fall for. And yeah, he'd noticed her, all right. He just wasn't sure yet whether that was a good or bad thing, because even though Kathleen seemed to think Sophie's debts and past behavior were no big deal, he was far from sure about that.

In his experience, women who needed funds—or, really, anyone who needed funds—looked to get them the easiest way possible. Which in this case meant through him.

The PDA beeped again, derailing his already chaotic thought process. He was down to two minutes.

Cursing, he dialed Martinez's number.

The sheriff picked up immediately. "Sophie?"

"No. It's Vaughn. I wanted—"

"What the hell took you so long to call?" the sheriff snapped, interrupting. "Where's Sophie? Is she okay?"

A massive chill crawled down Griffin's spine. "Why? What happened?"

"Didn't you get Ava's e-mail?"

Griffin cursed under his breath, remembering that the nasty-gram about Sophie's past had been the first of two in her inbox. "No. What have you got?"

"The prints weren't Perry's and they weren't Vince Del Gardo's. But they were in the system."

Griffin's gut tightened. "One of the construction crew?"

"No. A professional killer by the name of Boyd Perkins."

"A hitman?" Griffin snapped, disbelief racheting his volume up. "What the hell does a hitman have against me?"

"Not you. Del Gardo. Boyd Perkins often works for Nicky Wayne, head of the Wayne crime family in Las Vegas. They're the Del Gardo family's biggest competitors, and Nicky Wayne has hated Vince Del Gardo's guts ever since the botched contract kill that got Del Gardo convicted—Wayne was the target. If Perkins is up there, he's gunning after Del Gardo on behalf of Nicky Wayne."

"But why here?" Griffin demanded. But then, realizing that "why" wasn't the most important question, he said, "Never mind. Do you think Perry Long was working for this hitman?"

"Maybe. Or maybe he just got in the way and made a convenient body."

Griffin understood exactly where the sheriff was going with that, and his blood iced in his veins. They'd been fooled by a damned decoy, and Sophie was somewhere out in the mansion. Alone. Unprotected. He shot to his feet and hurried across the apartment. As he yanked on his borrowed boots, he snapped into the phone, "How long before you can get people up here?"

"It'll be at least three more hours before the skies clear."

Griffin cursed. "Get here as fast as you can. And bring dogs if you've got them. I think there are secret passages or something in this house, maybe in the mountain itself. If Del Gardo and Perkins are up here, playing cat-and-mouse, that's where they're hiding."

"Where's Sophie?"

The call was cut off before Griffin could respond to the sheriff's question, but he answered anyway, growling the words into the empty apartment. "I don't know, damn it. But I'm going to find her."

BOYD DUMPED the unconscious woman in the unfinished tunnel he'd chosen to serve as her and Vaughn's grave, then bent over her motionless form, cursing and pressing a hand to the wound in his side as he breathed through the pain.

He was a mess. His face hurt from the bruises Vaughn had pummeled into him the day before, and damned if he wasn't bleeding again. But at least his plan was working. It had needed a few necessary adjustments, granted, but it was working.

He'd arrived a week ago, and had arranged to bump into Perry Long at a bar down in Kenner City. A few beers and some negotiations, and Boyd had secured an invite up to Lonesome Lake, ostensibly as a newly hired worker, though Long believed he was a journalist trying to dig up dirt on the estate's prior owner, Vince Del Gardo.

Boyd had paid the contractor well for information about the estate, and had smirked when Perry had complained about the rash of accidents and setbacks the project had endured. That sort of thing was trademark Vince Del Gardo, and had only served to reinforce Boyd's conviction that his mark was hiding somewhere on the estate. The question was, where?

It hadn't been until just the day before the storm that the contractor had said something about the rumors that the estate was haunted. The workers had been going on about footsteps and missing tools and lunches, he'd said, inviting Boyd to laugh along with the joke. Only Boyd hadn't been laughing at all, because it made perfect sense. Del Gardo was a gutless rat. It figured he'd be hiding in the walls like a rodent. Once he knew what he was looking for, it hadn't taken much for him to find a way into one of the hidden passageways. After that, he'd just needed some uninterrupted time for searching. The blizzard had been convenient, offering him a few days when there would be no workers around, giving him ample opportunity to get in there, find Del Gardo, force him to divulge where he'd stashed the fifty million dollars he'd hidden from the government, and then kill him.

When the crew had cleared out of the mansion, Boyd had doubled back with his gear. He'd set up his camp in a high, shadowed nook of the barn and had been headed into the mansion for a first look-see when Perry's car had come screaming back up the driveway. Perry had been surprised to see him, but Boyd had made up some excuse about forgetting his notebook and Perry had been too preoccupied to care. He'd been in a dither because Griffin Vaughn, the rich-boy homeowner, was on his way up to see the project, and it was a mess.

Once Boyd had ascertained that there was no way Perry could talk Griffin Vaughn out of the visit, he'd walked him around the side of the building and tried to convince him to return to wait out the storm. Which would've worked fine, except that Del Gardo, apparently thinking the place would be deserted for the duration of the blizzard, had chosen that moment to walk by an upstairs window.

Perry had freaked, thinking the ghost was for real. Boyd had pulled his piece and shot out the window, aiming to wound so he could question Del Gardo about the missing fifty mil. He'd missed the bastard, cursed, and grabbed Perry before he could flee. Knowing he couldn't trust the contractor to keep his mouth shut, Boyd had broken Perry's neck and stashed him just inside the tunnel entrance he'd found in an outbuilding behind the main house. At the time he hadn't realized the body would prove useful; he'd just been looking for someplace inconspicuous to hide the corpse while he wired the bridge, figuring he could take out the richy-rich homeowner and Del Gardo's main escape route simultaneously.

But even the slickest plans sometimes had their kinks. Boyd hadn't realized until too late that Vaughn and his secretary had survived the explosion, and by the time he'd figured that out, the two had been firmly entrenched in the housekeepers' apartment. Since Boyd hadn't planned on tunnels or rock work, he'd only brought a limited amount of C4, which meant he couldn't simply blow the apartment. And once the blizzard hit, it had put a serious damper on any hope of sniping them through the windows. Besides, the guy, Vaughn, had skills. He'd covered the windows and set a perimeter, which had meant Boyd couldn't get to them easily. He'd had to wait for them to come to him.

Unfortunately, he hadn't expected to surprise them in the basement. It had been a miscalculation on his part to attack with nothing but a crowbar, but he hadn't realized the woman was armed. Worse, his 9 mm had jammed when he'd tried to fire, which meant his best recourse had been retreat.

The bitch had shot him in the back.

Scowling now, he nudged her motionless form with his toe. Not that he could blame her for the shot—he'd have done the same. And really, whichever way he looked at it, it was all business. It was his business to kill them, find Del Gardo and make his retrieval and his hit. And it was her business to try to stay alive, even if that meant shooting a man in the back.

Not that she knew she'd shot him. She thought she'd shot Perry, thanks to a little scene-setting and the extra bullet hole Boyd had put in the corpse and painted with his own blood. He'd thought it rather clever. And sure enough, Vaughn had dropped his guard, and he and the woman had split up. It would've been easier if Boyd could've captured Vaughn first and then gone after the secretary at his leisure, but things hadn't worked out that way, so he'd just have to improvise.

Humming softly, Boyd turned away from the woman and headed back for the surface. He had some more scene-setting to do.

SOPHIE WOKE SLOWLY, and for a long moment had no idea where she was or what had happened. All she knew was that it was very dark, she was very cold and she was lying on something hard, with her arms and legs twisted awkwardly behind her. She rolled and stretched, trying to work out the kinks, but her limbs didn't unkink. They were bound behind her.

Memory returned on a flash of pain and a scream that she choked off at the back of her throat. She remembered fighting with Griffin, and the memory brought a fresh wash of tears and pain. Worse, though, was the realization that she was in the exact situation they had tried so hard to avoid: in the power of the man who'd tried to kill them. But who could that be? Perry was dead. Maybe he hadn't been working alone; maybe the contractor had been nothing more than a decoy, she didn't know.

All she knew was that she was scared and alone, and she wanted Griffin. She didn't care if she got the soldier who'd protected her, the man who had loved her through the night, or the cynical businessman who had hurt her so deeply by not giving her a chance to defend herself against his accusations. He was a piece of all of those men—or more accurately, they were each a facet of his personality, all summing to the man who she trusted to get her out of danger, though she'd learned the hard way that she couldn't trust him with her heart.

"Damn it, Griffin," she muttered. "Where are you?" Surely he'd noticed by now that she wasn't in the mansion?

Not necessarily, a sly, hurtful voice whispered from

within her. And it was right, she realized. He'd been so furious with what he'd seen as her betrayal, that it was quite possible he wouldn't go after her until it was time to leave.

The thought that he might not even be looking for her was almost more than she could bear. Ever since they'd arrived at Lonesome Lake they'd been a team, coordinating their efforts and working together as best they could, despite—or maybe because of—the circumstances. And now all that was gone, taken from her by a nasty, rich woman who wanted to punish her for Tony's lies, and by the fact that Griffin couldn't find it in himself to trust her, or even listen to her side of the story.

Tears welled up and spilled over, tracking down Sophie's cheeks and cooling rapidly in the chill air. She couldn't see anything in the darkness, couldn't move, couldn't do anything, really.

Or could she? Her attacker hadn't gagged her, which suggested that he didn't think there was much of a chance that anyone would hear her if she screamed. But what if he was wrong?

Refusing to give up without a fight, she filled her lungs and cried out. She'd intended it to be a long, drawn-out scream, but what emerged instead was a single word. A name. "*Griffin!*"

CURSING STEADILY, fighting to keep from attacking the wall with his bare hands because he knew that wouldn't do a damn bit of good, Griffin worked his way around the basement, scanning each section of cement for evidence of a hidden doorway. He didn't see a damn thing, but there had to be a door, didn't there? Perkins had been in the basement one moment, gone then next. He'd vanished into thin air. But how the hell had he managed it?

Griffin pointed his flashlight down at the floor, looking for a trapdoor, a set of footprints—something, anything that would give him a clue. But the floor appeared to have been swept recently. That made sense if Perkins—or Del Gardo, for that matter—had been trying to hide evidence of foot traffic.

Which left Griffin exactly nowhere. It was nearly 1:00 p.m. and he hadn't seen Sophie since ten that morning. He knew where she'd been; he'd found scuff marks on the plywood subflooring, suggesting that there had been a struggle. The sight had hurt, deep inside him. The marks had been in the hallway just past the basement door, which had been unlocked when he was sure he'd locked it the day before. Which meant—

"Wait a minute." Griffin stopped dead as the pieces failed to line up. He knew he had secured the basement door, which only locked from the hallway side, not the side facing the stairs leading down. Which meant it'd been unlocked from inside the mansion. And that meant Perkins was using more than just the hidden entrance in the basement. He had to have some other way of getting into the mansion, at least one other access point. But where else had they seen evidence that they weren't alone?

Griffin racked his brain, thinking it through first as a

soldier, looking at it strategically. When that didn't get him anywhere, he tried to think it through analytically, as though it was a business deal. But that didn't work either.

"Damn it." He sank to his knees, kneeling on the cold, hard cement flooring of a basement that refused to give up its secrets. "Please. Where is she?" He didn't know who he was talking to, whether he was invoking some nebulous higher power, or trying to wrestle the information out of his own subconscious. "Where is Sophie?"

He thought of her as she'd been that morning, sleeping deeply amidst the rumpled covers. Her lips had been swollen from his kisses, her eyelids shadowed a delicate purple from lack of sleep, though she'd slept deeply once they'd finished with each other, replete and exhausted.

He'd wanted to go to her then; he'd wanted to touch her, to wake her, and tell her about his parents and the legend of the Vaughn virgin. He'd wanted to tell her all about Luke, about how he loved Spider-Man and video games, and called nearly every woman he met mama because he so wanted one of his own.

Instead, he'd decided to let her sleep. He'd gone into the kitchen and powered up the damn PDA, and everything had gone to hell. He still didn't know what to think about Sophie's debt or what had happened in her last job. But it didn't seem nearly so cut-and-dried as it had earlier that morning, when he'd decided to cut his losses, defend her against whatever came of Perry's death, and—

And that was it, he realized. Not Perry's death, but Perry himself. That was what his subconscious had been trying to tell him. His gut told him that Perkins had probably been the one to kill the contractor, and he'd set him near the woodshed as a decoy. Which meant Perkins himself had been somewhere near the woodshed.

Maybe even *in* the woodshed.

It was thin, Griffin knew, but he'd searched the basement thoroughly, to no avail. Rising to his feet, he sent a quick plea skyward, this time unashamedly aimed at the higher power he'd spent very little of his lifetime considering. "Please let her be okay. Please don't let me be too late."

With that, he took off for the woodshed at a dead run, charging up the basement stairs two at a time, and bursting out into the hallway. He slammed through the exterior door, and was instantly driven back against the wall of the mansion, lashed by storm winds that seemed, if anything, to have gotten worse than they'd been before.

Hoping to hell this was the blizzard's last dying gasp, Griffin fought the force of the driving snow, slogging one step at a time along the faint depression that showed where he and Sophie had walked the day before. Or maybe the track had been beaten down more recently— he couldn't tell. The windblown snow erased the evidence immediately, even wiping out his footprints almost as soon as he made them. He couldn't see Perry's body anymore; it had become the base for an enormous snow drift that covered almost one whole side of the shed.

When he reached the door leading to the shed, he thought a single word. *Please.* That was all. Just "please." Holding that prayer in his heart, he opened the woodshed door, braced for an attack and hoping he wouldn't see something far worse, like Sophie leaned up against the wall, frozen and still.

He got neither. The woodshed was just a woodshed— a ten-by-ten expanse with huge piles of split wood stacked in precise rows, with no deviation in the pattern. Except one.

Griffin's eyes were immediately drawn to a section in the corner, where the stacking seemed more haphazard than elsewhere, as though it'd been restacked far less precisely than elsewhere. Barely daring to hope, or to breathe, Griffin approached the section and shined his light all around the area.

The thin flashlight beam picked out a seam in the floor, a spot where the boards joined just slightly askew, forming a rectangular shape on the floor. A trapdoor.

Griffin's heart pounded in his chest, sending adrenaline through his system. He felt like the soldier now, and the man. He wanted to find Sophie, unharmed and alive. And he wanted to kill Perkins for daring to touch her.

Pulling the .45, which he'd tucked at the small of his back, he slipped the safety. Then, following a set of scuff marks in the sawdust, he pressed on a small, irregular section of flooring off to one side of the trapdoor.

The panel popped up soundlessly, working on a well-oiled mechanism.

Moving as quietly as he knew how, Griffin eased up the trapdoor. He shielded the light at first, listening intently in case Perkins was waiting for him down below. At first he heard nothing.

Then he heard a single word. His name, called softly in Sophie's voice.

He practically lunged through the trapdoor, but held himself in check and went step by step, testing the short ladder and the narrow passageway below, alert for traps. But all he found was a tunnel cut into the side of the mountain itself, running maybe fifty feet underground from the shed before it hit a T-intersection. One side dead-ended almost immediately. The other continued on beyond the reach of his flashlight beam, but he thought he saw movement just at the edge of the darkness.

Risking it because he couldn't stand it any longer, he whispered, "Sophie?"

"Griffin!"

He lunged toward her, weapon at the ready, but there was nobody to fight. She lay on the ground with her hands and feet bound behind her. Her face was pale, her lips bordering on blue. But her eyes were alight and alive, and filled with joy at the sight of him.

Relief hammered through him. What had happened between them earlier didn't matter right now. All that mattered was that she was okay, that he'd found her. They'd deal with the rest of it later.

"Sophie." He dropped to his knees beside her and yanked at the ropes, unknotting them quickly and freeing her. Then he dragged her up and into his arms, and hung on tightly as she sagged against him. "I was afraid I wouldn't get to you in time."

"So was I." Her voice trembled; her whole body trembled. "I wanted to have a chance to explain—"

"Me, too," he said, cutting her off. "Later, though. Let's get the hell out of here. The storm's almost over. The chopper should be cleared for takeoff in another hour or so."

She nodded against his throat. Keeping hold of her, he climbed to his feet and helped her up, and together they stagger-stepped along the tunnel toward the glow up ahead, where light filtered down through the opening.

They were maybe ten feet away when the trapdoor slammed shut.

"No!" Griffin shouted. He shoved the flashlight and .45 at Sophie, raced up the short ladder and slammed his shoulder into the panel, but to no avail. "Let us out!"

"Sorry, Vaughn," a man's voice said from up above. "I'd intended to finish you two off nice and neat right now, but I've just seen a rat pop his head out of a hidey hole. He's priority numero uno, so you'll have to wait."

There was a clattering roar as the hitman toppled one of the stacks of wood onto the trapdoor, weighing it down. Griffin roared a curse and shoved at the hatch, but it didn't budge upwards. If anything, it sagged down, bowing as the weight of the wood stressed the hinges and latch. There was no way Griffin could lift it from below.

Which meant they were caught in the tunnel, with no way out. Stuck there, waiting for the killer to return.

Chapter Ten

Sophie watched numbly as Griffin slammed his body up into the trapdoor twice more, following his progress by the thin flashlight beam.

She'd slipped the safety on the .45 and stuck the gun in her pocket, and held the light in both hands, clutching at the source of illumination. Even as dull shock reverberated through her at the realization that rescue had so quickly turned to renewed danger, she was pitifully grateful for light. She'd never thought of herself as afraid of the dark before, but she'd also never been tied up in a narrow dirt-and-stone tunnel before, either, left alone in the pitch darkness for hours in the freezing cold.

When Griffin sagged away from the trapdoor, breathing hard, she said softly, "You came looking for me. I wasn't sure you would."

"I don't blame you for wondering." He lifted his eyes to hers, and in the wan yellow light, she saw rage and regret, and a complicated mix of emotions she couldn't begin to identify. His jaw was darkly stubbled with the beginnings of a beard, and the tension coming off him in waves belonged entirely to the soldier. Yet there was an unusual gentleness about him as well, and she got the sense that although he was furious that he'd let their enemy get the drop on him, he was also aware of her, and worried for her. Worried about her.

In that moment he was both the soldier and the man who'd made love to her, and maybe even a little bit of the businessman who had judged her and found her lacking. He was all those things and more, the sum of the pieces becoming a larger whole.

She was unable to look away from his eyes, from the intensity of them and his searching gaze, which seemed to be simultaneously asking and telling her something, though she wasn't sure of either the question or information. She wanted to believe he'd come for her because he'd been worried, not because he'd felt it was his responsibility. But in the end, did it really matter? He'd come for her. That was the most important thing.

"Do you think there's another way out?" she asked softly.

"Perkins doesn't seem to think so."

"Who is Perkins?"

A humorless smile touched the corners of Griffin's mouth. "A hitman most likely on the trail of Vince Del Gardo, who, it appears, is still in the neighborhood after all. Perkins left the fingerprints you lifted off the crowbar. Which I would've known if I'd read both of the e-mails in your inbox, because Ava sent the info last night." He paused. "For what it's worth, I'm sorry."

For which part? she wanted to say, but couldn't

because there was too much information coming at her too quickly, and she didn't know what to focus on first.

Wobbling on legs made unsteady by the cold and lack of blood flow, along with shock, she let herself sag down to the tunnel floor, so she was leaning back against the rough rock surface of the tunnel wall. Griffin followed her down and sat cross-legged opposite her, facing her full-on. That was good because she could see his expression, but also bad, because she found she couldn't look away when he leaned in and touched a finger beneath her chin, tipping her eyes up to his.

"I'm sorry for missing the e-mail from Ava. If I'd gotten it, we would've known it wasn't safe for us to split up yet."

"But if Perkins left the fingerprints," she said, trying to work it through, "that means he was the man in the basement, right?"

"Right. The relative lack of blood on Perry's body bothered me at the time, but I didn't know enough to say for sure. With this added evidence, I think it's reasonable to figure that Perry was already dead, and Perkins shot him to mimic his own wound and get us to let our guard down."

If yesterday she'd had an inkling that she might be exonerated so thoroughly for Perry's death, she would've been relieved to the point of tears. Now, though, she felt only numbness. "And that was Perkins up there?"

Griffin nodded. "He mentioned a rat popping its head out. I'm guessing he saw Del Gardo and decided to go after him rather than finishing us off."

Sophie shivered at the thought. "So what do we do

now?" She pulled out the .45 and looked at it. "Wait until he comes back for us and try to kill him before he kills us?"

Three days earlier, it would've been unbelievable to think that she could say such a thing and mean it. But over the course of those three days, many things had changed.

"If necessary. I'd prefer to look for another way out, first. It doesn't make much sense to have a tunnel that doesn't lead anywhere."

"Unless it's more of a storage spot than a passage-way," she pointed out.

"Let's take a look and see."

Relieved to have even that small of a plan, Sophie stood when he did, handed over the .45, and moved to join him as he started testing the walls of the tunnel, sweeping his hands over the rough rock surface and pressing on any likely-looking bulges. She took the other side of the tunnel, and they worked their way from the ladder to where the tunnel branched to the left and right, but came up empty.

Griffin cursed and banged on the wall. "I bet this was supposed to go to the basement and join up with another hidden door."

"Another? You found the one he used the other day?"

"No, but I know it's there. I'm betting Del Gardo had them built. They could be anywhere, lead anywhere. Except for this one, which doesn't lead to a damn thing." His expression was hollow. Haunted.

Sophie wanted to touch him, to fold herself into his arms, but didn't know if she dared. Too much had been said between them, and even more had been left yet unsaid.

So instead of being weak when she so badly wanted

to be, she forced herself to think. The tunnel walls and ceiling were made of a mix of rock and soil. She asked, "Do you think we could dig our way out?"

Griffin thought about it for a long moment before shaking his head. "I don't think we dare. Even if we managed to punch through the permafrost—and that's a huge 'if'—we have no way of ensuring that we come out underneath a spot where the snow has blown thin. The last thing we need is for six feet of the stuff to come down on top of us and smother us to death. I'd rather take my chances fighting Perkins when he comes back, thank you."

"If he shot Perry to fake the wound, that means he's got a gun," she pointed out.

"So do I." But they both knew Perkins had the advantage. He could open up the trapdoor and fire down on them from above.

"Well, that's something, anyway." Sophie paused, taking stock and getting a glimmer of an idea. "So…you're the gadget guy, right? What do you think you could make out of the ropes I was tied with, plus the stuff we're wearing?" She was thinking along the lines of a pulley system or something, though wasn't clear on how that would help when what they really needed to do was push up on the trapdoor hard enough to break the door latch and shift the woodpile.

But a gleam kindled in Griffin's eyes. "I don't think I can do anything with the ropes or our clothes. The gun might be another story, though. The weight of the logs has already stressed the door…" He led the way back to the trapdoor, which had clearly buckled beneath the force pressing down on it from above. "If we can weaken the hinges or the latch enough, the wood might punch right through."

The awful pressure on Sophie's chest lightened a little. "You're going to shoot the door?"

He shook his head. "My aim would have to be dead-on, and the shot might still ricochet. I think it's too risky to use up the bullets that way."

"Then what?"

He pulled the .45, flipped open the cartridge and dumped the bullets into his palm. "Erik is a real do-it-yourselfer. He packs his own bullets, which probably means he adds a few extra grains of powder for more kick. It's what guys do. If I pull the grains out of the bullets, use the hammer and the caps to rig a detonator, I might be able to make some noise."

"You want to use the gun to build a mini-bomb and blow the trapdoor hinges?" Sophie asked, incredulous because it actually made sense. She stared at the metal cylinders resting in his palm. "Will six bullets be enough?"

"I've got another six in my pocket." Which wasn't really an answer.

"Can you hold a couple aside in case it doesn't work, and we need the gun for when Perkins comes back?"

"We could, but I'll need to disassemble the firing mechanism, too." His eyes were steady on hers. Soldier's eyes. "What do you think?"

He wouldn't do it if she objected, she knew. Fairness dictated that they both agree to effectively sabotaging their one means of defense, in the hopes of getting the heck out of there. So it was up to her.

She nodded slowly. "Let's do it."

He held her eyes for a long moment, as if assessing whether she really understood what she was agreeing to, and then tipped his head in acknowledgement. "I'll need you to hold the flashlight."

He dropped to sit cross-legged, pulled off his belt, and started using the tongue as a makeshift screwdriver to disassemble the .45. Sophie sat opposite him. She tried to follow his actions with the light, but found it difficult to minimize the shadows.

Worse, she had a feeling the batteries were on their way out. The cone of light, which had been yellow-white the day before, was headed more toward amber now. She could only hope they'd have enough light for Griffin to complete his work and get them out of there. God willing.

"Talk to me," he said absently. "Tell me a story."

"Any sort of story in particular?"

"How about the story of why you're nearly a hundred thou in debt and made yourself a powerful enemy."

She tensed. "Why now?"

"Kathleen. She told me that I should give you a chance to explain." He paused. "I was headed in that direction even before I talked to her, though. Things happened between us so quickly last night, and the situation in general has been so out of the norm, that there wasn't really time for you to tell me about it, was there?"

"It wasn't the first thing on my mind under the circumstances," she agreed, but something inside her was saying, *I wouldn't have told you regardless. It's my business, and I only asked you for one night.* Still, he was offering her an opportunity to explain Destiny's e-mail. It was what she'd wanted, what she'd begged him for earlier. And it was clear that he'd been hurt by finding out the way he had. He had lashed out, but there had been pain beneath the anger.

Deciding she owed it to herself, at least, to give him her side, she said, "My father died when I was very young, a month before he and my mother were supposed to get married. He'd been in the army, and died during a training exercise, but since they weren't married…" She lifted a shoulder. "No widows' benefits, no medical coverage."

Griffin frowned and glanced at her. "There are mechanisms in place to cover situations like that."

"Technically, yes. In reality, the people my mother contacted were very discouraging, telling her all the things she couldn't do rather than what she could. And her health was shaky even back then. The doctors gave it all sorts of names over the years, but none of them really stuck, and none of the treatments they tried worked for very long. She'd lost touch with her family—their fault, hers, I've never been sure, haven't been able to find them with the limited resources I've had access to." She lifted a shoulder. "When I was thirteen, it got to the point where she couldn't even get out of bed. Practically overnight, I went from being a normal kid to being a nurse."

"You could've gotten help," Griffin said bluntly. "You should've talked to a teacher, called DSS, something."

"I wasn't dropping the dime on my own mother. There were foster families in the apartments on either side of ours. Trust me, I was better off where I was." In the wan yellow light, she saw the dull horror on his face, and found herself resenting it. "Not such a pretty story, is it? So forgive me if I don't go around telling it to everyone I meet." She caught herself before she let rip with the deep resentment she carried toward people who worked within the system rather than trying to fix it. "Anyway, I learned the system as best I could, got her to as many doctors as I could, but none of it helped. My grades dropped, I missed lots of classes and eventually dropped out." Those years existed largely as a blur of days, chores, and crushing emotions. "I split my time between working crappy jobs that didn't cover all our expenses, keeping Mom comfortable, and going to the library, where I studied up on how to get the system to sit up and listen to me. Fast forward to eighteen months ago, when I finally, *finally* got her into a state-supplemented long-term care facility."

"Good for you." Griffin nodded that he understood, but how could he? He'd lost his parents, yes, but he'd had a long, happy childhood, and an uncle to lean on. She'd been completely on her own.

"Once she was being taken care of, I knew I had to find a job that would pay off our debts and cover my part of her care. But I'd been working mostly minimum-wage jobs, and never lasted more than a few months because I missed days dealing with her issues. How was I supposed to make headway on that sort of salary?

So I took a chance, took out some loans, and did a nine-month certificate in executive support."

"And went to work for Wade and Kane," Griffin said neutrally.

"That's not what you want to know about, though is it? You want to know about Tony. Fine. I worked with him, dated him, and would've slept with him first instead of you, if his fiancée hadn't shown up at the office, screaming bloody murder about the wedding and her daddy's money. It didn't matter to Destiny that I didn't know he was engaged, didn't matter that Tony had played her as much as he'd played me. She wanted me out of town before the wedding. Failing that, she wants me gone before the next election, when good old Tony plans to start his political career. I think Destiny lives in fear that one or more of his indiscretions is going to show up at an inconvenient time."

"With good reason, apparently." Griffin's tone and expression were unreadable. "She wrote the e-mail?"

"Yep. And leaned on her father's contacts to black-ball me pretty much citywide."

"Sounds like a charmer."

Sophie allowed herself a small smile. "Let's just say she and Tony deserve each other. And no, I won't be voting for him." It did feel a little better to have told Griffin the bare bones of the situation, she realized. And in telling it, she'd been reminded of the wide gap that existed between her and Griffin, not just in age and experience, but in their priorities. He'd done his service to his country. She was just gearing up to start. "And that, dear boss, is the long and short of it. I've got debts, yes, but they're my debts, and I'm not looking for someone to pay them off for me. Though I wouldn't say no to winning the lottery. And Tony…well, he was a mistake."

"Are we?" Griffin asked, focusing intently on the pile of parts he'd created from the disassembled .45.

"Are we what, a mistake?" She pinched the bridge of her nose, where a heck of a headache was forming. "Does it matter? It was just one night. Once we're out of here, it'll go back to business as usual. And if we don't make it out…well, it was just one night either way."

"What if I want it to be more?"

Something kicked in the region of her heart. "You swore off relationships, remember?"

"I've been reconsidering." His attention stayed on the creation that was taking shape beneath his quick, clever fingers, but she suspected his focus was as much an evasion as necessity. He continued, "There's a legend in my family. A correlation. Whatever you want to call it. Anyway, down through the generations, Vaughn men have had two types of marriages—absolute bliss or total disaster. The happy marriages, like my parents' and the one my Uncle Will is in now, have always involved a certain gap in age and experience, and have fallen along very traditional lines." He lifted one shoulder in a half shrug. "So I'll have to admit that the more we got to know each other over the past few days, the more I started to wonder if I'd been dating the wrong kind of woman. Or rather, if I'd been killing time, waiting for someone like you."

She stared at him, dumbfounded. "Is it my imagination, or did we just go from talking about a one-night stand to talking about marriage?"

"Obviously we'd have to spend more time together once we're out of here," he said, making it sound like a foregone conclusion, which she appreciated, even if the topic of conversation was making her twitchy and upset. "But yeah, I am. Which was one of the reasons I overreacted when I found out about your debt load and prior relationship. Except that wasn't fair, because I hadn't clued you into what I was thinking. I just figured, given the chemistry and the way we've been getting along, that you'd be interested in something longer term."

And she would've been, except that she wasn't entirely sure he wanted her. It seemed like he wanted an ideal, someone with her relative lack of experience in the bedroom, but with a similar lack of experience in other facets of life. Not to mention what he'd told her about his first marriage, and how he'd been looking for someone to keep his home and raise his son. Which wasn't wrong, necessarily. But she wasn't sure it was her.

He glanced over at her, expression wary. "Nothing to say?"

"I think…" She trailed off, trying to line it up in her head, struggling to figure out where the boundary between dreams and reality fell. "I think that if I believed you wanted a true partner, I'd be interested. But you said it yourself—you want a wife who will make you a home and help you raise Luke."

His hands stilled in the process of reassembling the

gun parts into something else entirely. He looked at her, eyes hooded. "What's wrong with that?"

"I have goals of my own, Griffin. Once I've paid off my debts and gotten ahead some, I'm serious about going to college, and from there to law school. I want to help people like my mother and me get the help they need."

He scowled and returned his attention to his project. "You don't need a law degree to advocate. Not if you've got VaughnTec money behind you."

Now it was her turn to go very, very still. After a moment, she said softly, "Yet you blame the other women for only wanting your money."

"Monique sold me her son," he bit off.

"But what about the others, Cara and the ones you've dated since? Did you ever stop to think that it wasn't so much them wanting the money, as much as it was the one thing you thought you could offer?"

It started coming clearer to her now. Clear and very sad. So much for her occasional thoughts that money could solve everything. Apparently, it just created a different set of problems.

"You made the company a success," she said softly, "but it didn't bring your parents back or save your marriage. You've bought this place, but it won't change the fact that Luke is growing up without a mother." She paused, aware that she'd not just stepped over the line, she'd shot and buried it. Since it was too late to retreat, and because she thought it needed to be said, she continued, "You don't want me, Griffin. You want some idealized version of what your parents had. I don't want that, not at this point in my life. I'm sorry."

Though she knew she was being as honest as she could, something tore in her chest at the words. She'd never known security, and had only really had a skewed version of love. Though Griffin hadn't said the word, she knew he'd primed himself for the emotion by slotting her into the family pattern. Would it really be so bad to live the life he could offer, and be loved by a man like him?

She didn't have an easy answer for that. All she knew was that she hadn't yet had a chance to live. Griffin was looking to make his world smaller at a time when hers had just begun to open up. One of these days she was going to get those debts paid off, and then, look out, world! She had a mark to make.

It was odd to realize that exhilaration could exist alongside heartache, but apparently it could. "I'm sorry," she whispered again, hating the pain she could see beneath his stern facade.

"Well. I guess that clears up a few things, doesn't it? My mistake."

"No," she said quickly. "No. It was…" But then she trailed off, because really, what could she say?

"It's okay. Really." He looked at her, and she saw from his eyes that he was trying to make it be okay. "I know I should be saying that I'd support whatever you want to do, that we can make it work. But I'm not sure that's in me. I want the Vaughn dream, Sophie. I want the wife and kids, the home cooking and the flowers on the table when I get home. And yeah, I know I can hire someone for most of that, but I don't want to. I want a woman who loves me so much that she just does stuff like that because she knows it'll make me happy, just like I'd do anything in my power to make her happy."

Except accepting that she wants to have a life of her own, Sophie thought. She didn't say it, though, because what would be the point? Instead, she said, "How's that contraption coming? We should probably get out of here."

He sent her a long look through shuttered eyes, then nodded. "Yeah," he said softly. "We probably should."

He stood, taking his makeshift mini-bomb with him, saying over his shoulder, "Come on. I'll need the light for this."

Trying to think of nothing but their escape plan, nothing but the moment at hand, Sophie held the dimming flashlight at a helpful angle as he affixed his device to the trapdoor. She didn't know what he'd done or how the thing was meant to work, but she didn't figure she needed to. What mattered was that he thought it was worth a shot.

She might not trust him to let her live her life, but she trusted him to save it, or die trying.

When he was done, he took her arm and urged her away. "We'd better get in the cross tunnel. I don't think the blast will reach that far, but better safe than sorry."

As they retreated from the immediate area of the trapdoor, he played out the rope she'd been bound with. One end of it was connected to the device, the other was looped around his wrist.

When they reached the T-intersection, he pushed her behind him and backed in, so she was shielded behind his big body.

Heart clutching a little at that quiet protection, she touched his arm and said softly, "I'm sorry. I wish things were different."

He held himself still for a long moment, before he exhaled a long breath and turned to face her. "Yeah. Me, too." He leaned down and touched his lips to hers in the briefest hint of a kiss. When he straightened away, he had a sad smile on his face. "For luck."

"For luck," she repeated, knowing that one way or the other, it would be their last kiss.

"Plug your ears," he said in warning. Moments later, he jerked on the rope.

There was a split-second pause, just long enough for her to fear that his device had failed. Then there was a sharp bang of detonation, followed by a huge crash.

"I think it worked!" He grabbed her and they hurried to the other end of the tunnel.

The air was thick with dust and a sharp, burning smell, but even as far back as the corner, they could see daylight up ahead. His plan had worked exactly as they had hoped; the trapdoor had given way and the logs had fallen through. He shoved the piled timber out of the way, then grabbed one stick and held it as a makeshift club as he scrambled partway up, stuck his head through the opening, and took a cautious look around. Moments later, he ducked back down and waved to her. "It looks okay. Come on."

She grabbed on to his outstretched hand. He helped her scramble up the teetering pile of logs, and kept hold of her hand as they headed across the woodshed. Sophie didn't mind the grip, though, because it anchored her in a world that suddenly seemed far too bright.

She blinked, figuring it was because of the difference between the dark tunnel and the gray light of day. But when her vision cleared, she didn't see grayness at all. Through the open door of the woodshed, she saw a patch of dazzling white snow, a drift-shrouded corner of the mansion…and blue sky.

The blizzard had passed.

Griffin turned to her, expression guarded. "Two sets of tracks lead into the mansion, one from this building, one from around the side. I don't think we dare try heading for the house or we'll risk getting caught in the crossfire. But that might play in our favor, too, because if Perkins is preoccupied with tracking his mark and figures we're pinned down in the tunnel, he might not be keeping an eye on the driveway. What do you say we make a run for it, heading downhill, and meet the chopper on its way up from the city?"

Sophie sucked in a breath past the huge lump her heart had made in her throat. Some part of her must have thought that once they made it out of the tunnel, and once the storm passed, they'd be home free. But they weren't. He was right. They couldn't go back to the mansion, couldn't stay where they were. But there was a very real flaw in his plan. "What if the helicopter gets delayed, or another snow squall blows up?" They would be stuck out in the open, with no supplies or protection.

Griffin held her eyes with his. "I promise I'll do whatever I can to keep you safe."

He'd made the same promise to her before, as they had struggled up the driveway, wet and cold and shivering, not realizing that their problems were just beginning. She had believed him then, and she believed him even more deeply now. Griffin was a good man, a man of his word, and she trusted him implicitly.

The realization gave her pause, because if that were the case, then why had she so thoroughly rejected the thought of a future with him? He was a proud and stubborn man, yes, but he was also rational. A businessman as well as a warrior. If he came to love her, and they decided to make a life together, it would be a negotiation, not a dictatorship. Maybe, just maybe, in this case she was the one who had knee-jerked a response based on her own past. What if, in an effort to protect her own freedom, she was in danger of throwing away something that would make that freedom so much better?

"Griffin…" she began, but then trailed off, because now was neither the time nor the place. "Never mind." She squeezed her fingers on his. "I trust you. Down the hill we go."

He looked at her intently as though he, too, wanted to say something more. But in the end, he simply nodded and said, "Stay close."

They came out the door hand-in-hand and hit the ground running. The snow had blown mostly clear to one side of the shed and they headed that way, moving fast and aiming downhill. As they cleared the woodshed, Sophie caught a blur of motion out of the corner of her eye, but it was already too late.

A rough hand grabbed her and yanked her back, tearing her hand from Griffin's. A strong forearm clamped across her throat and cool metal touched her temple. A gun.

"Griffin!" she screamed, fearing that this time not even he would be able to save her.

Chapter Eleven

Griffin spun and nearly launched himself at the man who held Sophie, but froze the instant he saw the gun. Very slowly he dropped the firewood club and raised both hands, palms out, showing that he was unarmed.

The man who held Sophie was in his early forties, bareheaded and bald, with strong features and the cold blue eyes of a killer. He was wearing a winter camouflage snowsuit and held a 9mm to Sophie's temple with the ease of familiarity. His age matched that of hired killer Boyd Perkins, not fugitive mobster Vince Del Gardo. Which meant that maybe, just maybe, the hitman could be bought with a better offer.

"Think it through," Griffin said calmly. "I've got money, and the only thing I want to do is get the hell out of here, and take my assistant with me." He deliberately downgraded Sophie to her professional role, lest Perkins use their relationship as added leverage.

Because they *did* have a relationship, damn it, and he was going to do whatever it took to make sure that relationship had a chance of moving forward. Fairness forced him to admit—inwardly, at least—that she was right about some things. Maybe he had been trying to fit the women in his life into the mold of the Vaughn virgin and his parents' marriage. But if he could admit it then he could work to change it, if that was what it took to keep Sophie in his life.

Perkins smirked faintly at the offer of a bigger buyout. "Sorry, Mr. Vaughn. I stay bought, and I can't afford witnesses."

His finger tightened infinitesimally on the trigger in prelude to the killing shot. Griffin lunged forward, his heart stopping dead in his chest, shouting, "No!"

Perkins shifted to avoid the charge. As he did so, Sophie drove her elbow into his right side, just above his hip.

The hitman shouted in pain and staggered back. Griffin grabbed Sophie and ripped her away from the other man a split second before the gun roared. The bullet sang harmlessly into the trees as Griffin fell on Perkins, shouting.

Rage suffused Griffin, along with a territorial possessiveness he'd never experienced before. He pummeled the bastard, hammering him with his fists for scaring Sophie, for threatening her. For nearly killing her. The hitman fought back, but he was favoring his injured side. Griffin took ruthless advantage of the fact, digging his knee into the spot and landing a roundhouse punch when Perkins screamed in pain.

Griffin yanked the 9 mm from the hitman's lax fingers, and tossed the gun in Sophie's direction. "Take this." He didn't want Perkins getting it back and didn't want to hold it himself because it'd be a serious temptation to use it on the bastard.

Then he dragged Perkins to his feet and got in the dazed, semiconscious man's face. "Let's see how you like being tied up and stuck in a hole for a few hours while we wait for the sheriff!"

He was dragging Perkins toward the woodshed when he heard Sophie scream, "Griffin, look out!"

She started racing toward him, struggling through the snow, her attention fixed on an upper floor of the mansion.

Griffin jerked his head up just in time to see a glint of metal and motion from the broken second-story window. Screaming his name, Sophie threw herself at him just as the crack of a high-powered rifle echoed in the crisp winter air.

She slumped and crashed into him as deadweight, driving him to his knees. He lost his grip on Perkins, who ripped away from him and fled. Two more rifle shots sounded in quick succession, both missing Perkins, who disappeared into the tree line behind the woodshed.

Then, as Griffin had known he would, the man in the second-story window trained his rifle on him and Sophie. *No witnesses*, Perkins had said, and the same held true for the second man. Griffin couldn't see his features, but had to assume it was Del Gardo.

Griffin ducked and braced himself, trying to cover as much of Sophie's still form as he could with his own body.

"Go!" he thought he heard her say.

"I'm not leaving you," he growled. "Not ever." He closed his eyes and waited for the sound of a gunshot.

Instead he heard the rhythmical thump of a helicopter's rotors. Moments later, a small, light chopper came over the tree line, proudly bearing the VaughnTec logo on its doors. Help had arrived!

There was a swirl of motion as Del Gardo shouldered the rifle and disappeared from the window.

Griffin barely noticed, though. His entire focus was locked on the woman in his arms.

Sophie's exertion-flushed face was rapidly draining to waxen with pain and shock. He held her close, and didn't have to look to know that the warm wetness on his hands was her blood. She'd been shot pushing him out of the line of fire. She had, quite literally, taken a bullet for him.

"Hang on," he said urgently. "The cavalry's here. We'll get you back to Kenner City pronto and get you patched up. Just think, fresh food and hot water. Come on, stay with me. You don't want to miss out on a burger and a shower, do you?"

In response to his nonsense, her eyelids fluttered and then lifted, and her light brown eyes focused on him. The corners of her lips trembled. "You're okay."

That brought it all crashing down around him. A moan of pain ripped from his throat, and came out sounding like a sob. "I shouldn't be. You never should've gotten in the way. I'm the one who's supposed to protect you."

She started to say something, but broke off when her breath rattled in her lungs. She coughed slightly, bringing a wince of pain and spots of blood to her lips. The sight just about broke his heart, and when she tried to talk again, he shushed her with a kiss. "Hush. We can talk later."

She shook her head. "What if there isn't a later?" Her words were stronger now, as though she'd found another reserve, or was reaching the end of it. "If I've learned anything over the last few days, it's that we shouldn't assume there's going to be a tomorrow."

"But I want there to be," Griffin said, feeling it all start to slip away from him. As close to panicking as he'd ever been before in his life, he said, "I'll do anything, give anything to make sure there's a future for us."

"I believe you," she said, and his heart shuddered in his chest when he saw the sheen of love and acceptance in her eyes. "I was wrong before."

"No, I was."

"Fine, we both were. The thing is, I do want a future with you. I don't know how we'll make it work, but I want to try."

"It's a deal," Griffin whispered as her eyelids fluttered shut once again. He kissed her cheeks, then her lips, not a soldier or a tycoon now, but simply a man who held his woman in his arms and prayed that that he hadn't found her only to lose her that same day. Pressing close to her, he whispered, "Why did you take that bullet?"

He didn't expect an answer, but he got one, a thready whisper of, "Because this isn't about you protecting me. It's about us being a team."

That was the last thing she said.

The helicopter landed nearby and Sheriff Martinez

leaped out, followed by a half dozen others, which was more than the small chopper was rated for.

Griffin gathered Sophie in his arms and lifted her, trying not to see how much blood had spread in the snow beneath them. As he carried her limp form to the waiting helicopter, he called to the sheriff, "You'll see Perkins's trail leading off behind the woodshed, and Del Gardo was in the upstairs bedroom with the broken window no more than three minutes ago. Do whatever you need to do with my property, I don't care. Just find the bastards."

Then he climbed into the chopper with Sophie, barking for the copilot to get the first aid kit, pronto. The pilot had them in the air in no time flat, radioing ahead to find the nearest hospital helipad and warn the emergency doctors of an incoming gunshot victim. Griffin leaned over Sophie, talking to her, trying to stop the copious blood flow that was coming from a bullet wound in her upper chest.

He was wholly focused on the woman who in a few short days had become, in his heart at least, part of his family. He glanced back once as the helicopter flew away from Lonesome Lake, and saw the investigators fanning out in search of Boyd Perkins. A part of him wished he'd killed the bastard himself, but another, more civilized part of him was content to leave it to Martinez and his people. It was time to begin a new chapter in his life. Starting now.

Leaning down, he brushed a tendril of dark blond hair from Sophie's brow, and whispered, "Hang in there, beautiful. You can do it. You can do anything you want."

SOPHIE FLICKERED in and out of consciousness for what seemed like a long time, though her sense of time felt seriously out of whack, as did the rest of her body. She was light-headed and giddy half the time, crushed with pain the other half. She barely knew her own name, never mind where she was, or why. The only thing she did know for sure, the only constant she came to rely on, was the presence of the big, solid man at her bedside, his silver-shot hair standing up in finger-rumpled spikes, and his eyes tired and full of worry.

Griffin was there constantly, day and night. When she opened her eyes, he whispered words of praise and love, or updated her on what was happening in the outside world, though she didn't retain any of it when she slipped back under again.

Then, finally, she woke all the way and felt clear-headed, though weak and sore. It was daylight, though she couldn't have said what day, and Griffin was there, moving into her line of sight immediately, his mesmerizing green eyes full of hope. "Hey. How are you feeling?"

"Capable of speech, which is an improvement," her words came out barely above a whisper, and the effort sent a twinge of pain through her chest, but all of that was still better than it had been.

As her eyes adjusted, she became aware that they weren't alone. Sheriff Martinez stood at the end of the bed, next to a wiry, light-complexioned stranger with black hair, piercing blue eyes and a scar on his chin.

"Hey, Sheriff," she said, her voice sounding a little stronger this time. "Did you get Perkins?"

She saw the answer in Martinez's frustrated expression, but it was the other man who spoke, saying, "Ms. LaRue, my name is Dylan Acevedo. I'm with the FBI. We were just starting to discuss our findings with Mr. Vaughn here. Is it okay if we continue? Then, if you're up to it, maybe you could answer a couple of questions?"

Griffin shook his head and moved toward the men. "I don't think—"

"Wait." She caught Griffin's hand. "I'd like to hear what they have to say."

He stopped, but shot her a dark, disgruntled look. "You had a bullet taken out of your right lung. You think you could maybe take it easy for a day or two?"

Though her heart stuttered a little at the confirmation that she'd been seriously injured, though she'd already guessed it from the number of monitors and the length of time she'd been incoherent, she squeezed his fingers. "I promise that if it's too much, I'll either kick them out or fall asleep on you guys mid-sentence."

She was pretty sure she'd done the latter a couple of times in recent days. The corners of his mouth twitched, confirming it. "Okay. You win." His eyes warmed a notch. "Guess I'd better get used to that, huh?"

Her pulse kicked at the reminder of the things they'd said to each other up at Lonesome Lake, but she figured that was a conversation better held in private, so she looked back to Sheriff Martinez and Agent Acevedo. "Go on. I think you've got at least five minutes before I conk out again."

The agent inclined his head. "Then to keep it short, Mr. Vaughn here has already confirmed from a photo lineup that Boyd Perkins was the man who attacked and imprisoned the two of you. All of the evidence collected from the estate, by myself as well as Callie and Ava, indicates the presence of two men—Perkins, and another man whose height and weight are roughly consistent with that of Vince Del Gardo. Unfortunately, both of the men remain at large, and the second storm meant we weren't able to bring up the equipment needed to find any other access tunnels."

Sophie made a face and glanced at Griffin. "Another storm?"

He nodded. "At least this time we're in Kenner City where we belong."

"Actually, I'm pretty sure we belong in San Francisco."

He lifted a shoulder. "I had Hal take the jet and pick up Darryn and Luke. They're here now, which makes it feel a lot more like home."

Sophie searched his eyes, trying to interpret the undercurrents in that statement, and failing.

"What we were hoping to get from you," Martinez said, redirecting her attention, "is a description of Del Gardo."

She frowned. "You don't know what he looks like?"

"There's some speculation that he may have changed his appearance through plastic surgery. We were thinking you might be able to give us something more to go on."

"Sorry." She shook her head, though it was starting to throb as she hit the end of her small reserve of strength. "I just saw movement, and the rifle. A man's figure in the broken window. Nothing else."

"That's all I saw, too," Griffin said, gripping her hand in support. He looked over at the sheriff and FBI agent. "I think that's enough for her for now."

Sophie didn't protest, because she was already sliding toward sleep.

When she awoke next, she looked automatically to the chair beside her bed. For the first time since she'd woken up in the hospital, Griffin wasn't there. In his habitual place sat a slick, cool-looking blond woman in her mid-thirties. Beside her, in a second visitor's chair, sat a petite redhead with porcelain skin and vivid blue eyes. Both of them were wearing street clothes, but the blonde had a badge hung around her neck, identifying her as a member of the KCCU.

At first, Sophie assumed they were there to ask her more questions. But the air between the two women crackled with excitement, and their eyes shone, making Sophie think that something other than business had woken her. "What's up?" she asked, figuring that was more polite than leading with, *Who the heck are you?* For all she knew, she'd met the women earlier during her recovery and had blanked on it.

"Welcome back to the land of the living," the blonde said. "I'm Callie and this is Ava. You talked to us on the phone from Lonesome Lake? We wanted to meet you in person after all that long-distance stuff. And we wanted to let you know that if you're ever looking for a job, you might think of crime scene analysis. That was a hell of a set of fingerprints for using pancake makeup and packing tape!"

Sophie laughed, feeling the same instant connection to the two women that she'd felt during their phone conversations. "I'm happy to put faces to the voices! Now, tell me what I just missed. I'm guessing it was something big."

Ava's eyes sparkled. "I was just telling Callie that Ben—that'd be FBI agent Ben Parrish—just proposed, and we're going to tie the knot this weekend!"

"Wow," Sophie said. "Congratulations!"

Ava patted her stomach, drawing Sophie's attention to the gentle swell of a baby bump. "I know it's pretty hurry-up on the wedding end of things, but we're sort of doing this out of order."

Sophie smiled shyly, feeling more than a little out of her element as she realized that, just as she'd gone a long time without a man in her life, it'd been years since she'd had any real female friends to speak of. "Congratulations. Really." She glanced at Callie, who seemed to be the more reserved of the two. "Is there any news on the investigation?" Sophie faltered. "I mean, that you can tell me about? If you can't it's no big deal. It's just—" She broke off and blew out a frustrated breath. "Never mind. It's just that you guys made me feel like one of the team when we were on the phone together. I have to remember it's back-to-reality time."

Callie grinned. "You'll find we're a fairly relaxed group. Within reason, of course. So I'll tell you that we've got a ton of questions and no real answers right now. Given the amount of snow the second storm dumped on the mountains, there's not much we can do up at

Lonesome Lake at the moment. And yeah, we liked talking with you, too. That's part of why we're here. We wanted to put in a vote that you and your hunky millionaire boyfriend, and his super adorable kid, should stick around. Maybe not up at Lonesome Lake, at least not until we've fully cleared it. But maybe in Kenner City."

Sophie felt the prickly heat of a blush cover her cheeks. "My boyfriend, huh? Seems like a strange term for a guy who's…well, not a boy."

That got some eyebrow wiggles from her new friends, but any further conversation was interrupted by the sound of male voices in the hallway, followed by the door swinging open. Griffin stood in the doorway, with Luke at his side. Luke was gripping a file folder with careful concentration.

"I think that's our cue." Callie rose, pausing to jot something on the bedside pad. "That's my number. If you're going to be in town for a while, give me a call and we can get together some time."

The women filed out, greeting Griffin and tousling Luke's hair on the way by. When the door swung shut at their backs, Sophie used the remote control to raise the head of her bed, allowing her to sit partway up.

A quiver took root in the pit of her stomach, warning her that this could be a major moment in progress. The thing was, she didn't know which way it was going to go. She and Griffin had connected up at Lonesome Lake, but how much of what they'd said to each other had stuck once his helicopter had dropped him back in reality?

Sure, he'd stayed by her side, and yes, he'd hinted at there being a future for them, even in front of the sheriff and Agent Acevedo. But what shape would that future take? Would Griffin try to ease her into the role of his fantasy wife, or would he be open to negotiating?

Unable to guess any of the answers from his expression, she said, "Hey, guys." Then, focusing on the child at Griffin's side, she said, "Hi, Luke. I'm…" She faltered, knowing that one of Griffin's biggest hang-ups was his son getting too attached too quickly. "I'm Sophie."

Luke, who even with short blond hair and brown eyes somehow managed to look like a miniature version of Griffin, looked up at his father. "Now, Dad?"

"Yeah," Griffin said, his voice soft and a little rough. "Now would be good." He kept his eyes fastened on her as Luke crossed the room, stopped near Sophie's beside and held out the file folder. "These are for you."

"Thank you." She took the file, though she hadn't a clue what it contained. His job completed, Luke scampered back to his father's side.

Griffin, however, crossed the room and took his usual seat, then hoisted his son up onto his lap. Griffin was wearing jeans and a cable-knit sweater the same color as his eyes, and he seemed far more relaxed than she'd ever seen him before. He wasn't the soldier, the tycoon or the lover now. He was the father. The family man.

And somehow she instinctively knew this was the man she'd been trying to find inside him all along. The man who was brought to the fore by his son. But it wasn't his son he was looking at right now with all the love in the world plain for her to see in his eyes.

No, he was looking at her.

"Open it," he said. "And please do me a favor and hear me out before you get mad."

"Oh, well. With a lead-in like that…" Faint butter-flies churned in her stomach as she flipped open the file.

The first page was a terse e-mail sent from Tony's account at Wade & Kane. All it said was, "Done."

She glanced at Griffin. "What's done?"

His eyes hardened to those of the soldier. "I told both he and his wife that they would sorely regret it if they ever contacted, spoke or even thought about you ever again." He paused. "And if you want to accuse me of throwing my weight around, then yes, that's exactly what I did. But she started it."

"Yes, she certainly did." Sophie tried not to feel a slice of satisfaction that he'd dealt with Destiny in such a way. She failed, because it *was* satisfying. "Sometimes it just takes the right weapon to do the job." She smiled at him, sharing her approval with Luke. "Thank you both."

"Keep going," Griffin said. "Or better yet, let me explain first."

"Okay, now I'm nervous."

"Trust me, not nearly as nervous as I am." And for the first time since she'd known Griffin, he looked less than a hundred percent confident.

"You're not going to drop coffee on me, are you?"

"I'll try not to." He blew out a breath. "Here goes. I've cleared your debts. All of them." He held up a hand to keep her from interrupting, not seeming to understand that all the breath had just left her lungs. "I know you didn't want me to, and you're probably thinking I did it to control you, or make you feel like you owe me, or something like that. And I could see how it might look that way. But I'd really rather you consider it hazardous duty pay for me dragging you up to Lonesome Lake. Anything but an effort to make our relationship into something other than a fifty-fifty partnership."

It wasn't until the last sentence that the pressure in her chest eased. Those, it seemed, were the magic words. "Fifty-fifty, eh?" She arched an eyebrow. "And what, exactly, am I going to be doing with my fifty percent of this relationship?"

"Whatever you want," he said with quiet simplicity. "If you want to go to law school, I'll pack your lunch. So to speak, anyway. What you saw up at the mansion was about the sum total of my cooking skills. On the other hand, if you want to use our money to springboard yourself straight to advocacy, or open an office that employs a half dozen lawyers dedicated to your cause, then that's what we'll do. Hell, I don't care if you want to knit doilies or run for President. I'll support you no matter what."

All of a sudden, it sounded too big, too huge for someone like her. "I don't know if I can do all that."

"Then we'll do it together," he said. "All I'm asking is that you stick around and get to know Luke and me as a family, and Darryn, because he's family, too. And that while you're doing that, you consider marrying us."

Her throat closed and her eyes filled with tears. "I will."

He went very still. "You will what? Stick around, or marry us?"

"Both," she said, and there wasn't a single qualm in her heart. "I love you."

His features eased, as though he'd been braced for something else. As though he'd feared that even after all they'd been through together, the family of his dreams would stay beyond his reach. Exhaling on a gusty sigh, he said, "And I love you."

Bringing Luke with him, he leaned over the bed and kissed her, very gently, still mindful of her injuries.

Sophie wept a little and clung, and couldn't help thinking that not in a million years would she have predicted this based on her first day of work, when he'd scowled at her and she'd dumped a pot of coffee in his lap. But it turned out that Kathleen had been right, even though neither of them had known the retiree had been matchmaking. It might have taken them a three-day blizzard and harrowing danger to figure it out, but in the end, the reality was inescapable.

They were a perfect fit.

* * * * *

*The blizzard may be over but there's
plenty of danger left in Kenner County.
Don't miss CRIMINALLY HANDSOME,
the next book in the
KENNER COUNTY CRIME UNIT series,
by Cassie Miles.
Only from Harlequin Intrigue!*

Celebrate 60 years of pure reading pleasure with Harlequin®!

Silhouette® Romantic Suspense is celebrating with the glamour-filled, adrenaline-charged series LOVE IN 60 SECONDS starting in April 2009.

Six stories that promise to bring the glitz of Las Vegas, the danger of revenge, the mystery of a missing diamond, family scandals and ripped-from-the-headlines intrigue. Get your heart racing as love happens in sixty seconds!

Enjoy a sneak peek of
USA TODAY bestselling author Marie Ferrarella's
THE HEIRESS'S 2-WEEK AFFAIR
Available April 2009 from Silhouette® Romantic Suspense.

Eight years ago Matt Shaffer had vanished out of Natalie Rothchild's life, leaving behind a one-line note tucked under a pillow that had grown cold: *I'm sorry, but this just isn't going to work.*

That was it. No explanation, no real indication of remorse. The note had been as clinical and compassionless as an eviction notice, which, in effect, it had been, Natalie thought as she navigated through the morning traffic. Matt had written the note to evict her from his life.

She'd spent the next two weeks crying, breaking down without warning as she walked down the street, or as she sat staring at a meal she couldn't bring herself to eat.

Candace, she remembered with a bittersweet pang, had tried to get her to go clubbing in order to get her to forget about Matt.

She'd turned her twin down, but she did get her act together. If Matt didn't think enough of their relationship to try to contact her, to try to make her understand why he'd changed so radically from lover to stranger, then to hell with him. He was dead to her, she resolved. And he'd remained that way.

Until twenty minutes ago.

The adrenaline in her veins kept mounting.

Natalie focused on her driving. Vegas in the daylight wasn't nearly as alluring, as magical and glitzy as it was after dark. Like an aging woman best seen in soft lighting, Vegas's imperfections were all visible in the daylight. Natalie supposed that was why people like her sister didn't like to get up until noon. They lived for the night.

Except that Candace could no longer do that.

The thought brought a fresh, sharp ache with it.

"Damn it, Candy, what a waste," Natalie murmured under her breath.

She pulled up before the Janus casino. One of the three valets currently on duty came to life and made a beeline for her vehicle.

"Welcome to the Janus," the young attendant said cheerfully as he opened her door with a flourish.

"We'll see," she replied solemnly.

As he pulled away with her car, Natalie looked up at the casino's logo. Janus was the Roman god with two faces, one pointed toward the past, the other facing the future. It struck her as rather ironic, given what she was doing here, seeking out someone from her past in order to get answers so that the future could be settled.

The moment she entered the casino, the Vegas phenomenon took hold. It was like stepping into a world where time did not matter or even make an appearance. There was only a sense of "now."

Because in Natalie's experience she'd discovered that bartenders knew the inner workings of any establishment they worked for better than anyone else, she made her way to the first bar she saw within the casino.

The bartender in attendance was a gregarious man in his early forties. He had a quick, sexy smile, which was probably one of the main reasons he'd been hired. His name tag identified him as Kevin.

Moving to her end of the bar, Kevin asked, "What'll it be, pretty lady?"

"Information." She saw a dubious look cross his brow. To counter that, she took out her badge. Granted she wasn't here in an official capacity, but Kevin didn't need to know that. "Were you on duty last night?"

Kevin began to wipe the gleaming black surface of the bar. "You mean during the gala?"

"Yes."

The smile gracing his lips was a satisfied one. Last night had obviously been profitable for him, she judged. "I caught an extra shift."

She took out Candace's photograph and carefully placed it on the bar. "Did you happen to see this woman there?"

The bartender glanced at the picture. Mild interest turned to recognition. "You mean Candace Rothchild? Yeah, she was here, loud and brassy as always. But not for long," he added, looking rather disappointed. There was always a circus when Candace was around, Natalie thought. "She and the boss had at it and then he had our head of security escort her out."

She latched onto the first part of his statement. "They argued? About what?"

He shook his head. "Couldn't tell you. Too far away for anything but body language," he confessed.

"And the head of security?" she asked.

"He got her to leave."

She leaned in over the bar. "Tell me about him."

"Don't know much," the bartender admitted. "Just that his name's Matt Shaffer. Boss flew him in from L.A., where he was head of security for Montgomery Enterprises."

There was no avoiding it, she thought darkly. She was going to have to talk to Matt. The thought left her cold. "Do you know where I can find him right now?"

Kevin glanced at his watch. "He should be in his office. On the second floor, toward the rear." He gave her the numbers of the rooms where the monitors that kept watch over the casino guests as they tried their luck against the house were located.

Taking out a twenty, she placed it on the bar. "Thanks for your help."

Kevin slipped the bill into his vest pocket. "Any time, lovely lady," he called after her. "Any time."

She debated going up the stairs, then decided on the elevator. The car that took her up to the second floor was empty. Natalie stepped out of the elevator, looked around to get her bearings and then walked toward the rear of the floor.

"Into the Valley of Death rode the six hundred," she silently recited, digging deep for a line from a poem by Tennyson. Wrapping her hand around a brass handle, she opened one of the glass doors and walked in.

The woman whose desk was closest to the door looked up. "You can't come in here. This is a restricted area."

Natalie already had her ID in her hand and held it up. "I'm looking for Matt Shaffer," she told the woman.

God, even saying his name made her mouth go dry. She was supposed to be over him, to have moved on with her life. What happened?

The woman began to answer her. "He's—"

"Right here."

The deep voice came from behind her. Natalie felt every single nerve ending go on tactical alert at the same moment that all the hairs at the back of her neck stood up. Eight years had passed, but she would have recognized his voice anywhere.

* * * * *

*Why did Matt Shaffer leave heiress-turned-cop
Natalie Rothchild?*
*What does he know about the death of Natalie's
twin sister?*
*Come and meet these two reunited lovers and learn
the secrets of the Rothchild family in*
THE HEIRESS'S 2-WEEK AFFAIR
by USA TODAY *bestselling author*
Marie Ferrarella.
*The first book in Silhouette® Romantic Suspense's
wildly romantic new continuity,*
LOVE IN 60 SECONDS!
Available April 2009.

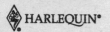
HARLEQUIN®
INTRIGUE®

B.J. DANIELS

FIVE BROTHERS
ONE MARRIAGE-PACT
RACE TO THE HITCHING POST

WHITEHORSE
MONTANA
The Corbetts

SHOTGUN BRIDE

Available April 2009

Catch all five adventures in
this new exciting miniseries
from B.J. Daniels!

The Inside Romance newsletter has a NEW look for the new year!

Same great content, brand-new look!

You're invited to join our Tell Harlequin Reader Panel!

By joining our new reader panel you will:

- Receive Harlequin® books—they are FREE and yours to keep with no obligation to purchase anything!
- Participate in fun online surveys
- Exchange opinions and ideas with women just like you
- Have a say in our new book ideas and help us publish the best in women's fiction

In addition, you will have a chance to win great prizes and receive special gifts!
See Web site for details. Some conditions apply.
Space is limited.

To join, visit us at
www.TellHarlequin.com.

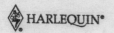

INTRIGUE

COMING NEXT MONTH
Available April 14, 2009

#1125 SHOTGUN BRIDE by B.J. Daniels
Whitehorse, Montana: The Corbetts
A former Texas Ranger is not prepared to fall for a blue-eyed Montana cowgirl who has had enough of heartbreak. When her troubling past leads to her abduction, is he ready to ride to her rescue?

#1126 CRIMINALLY HANDSOME by Cassie Miles
Kenner County Crime Unit
A terrifying vision sends a frightened psychic into the protective arms of a skeptical CSI expert. To catch a killer, they will need to work together—closely.

#1127 BABY BLING by Elle James
Diamonds and Daddies
Two months ago, Houston's shipping tycoon slept with the one woman he should have left alone—his assistant and friend. Now he needs her help to stop terrorists, and she needs to tell him she is pregnant!

#1128 RESCUING THE VIRGIN by Patricia Rosemoor
The McKenna Legacy
An undercover special agent is shocked when he discovers a beautiful American woman trapped by the human-trafficking ring he is trying to bring down. Can he save her and bring the mastermind behind the scheme to justice?

#1129 A STRANGER'S BABY by Kerry Connor
With the help of the handsome man next door, she is unraveling the sinister truth behind the one-night stand that left her pregnant and alone. Now that someone is threatening her baby and safety, can they find out the truth before it is too late?

#1130 BULLETPROOF TEXAS by Kay Thomas
To extract cancer-eating bacteria from a flooding cave, a research scientist accepts the help of a laid-back caving guide. But a psychopathic competitor decides this potential cure shouldn't see the light of day—and is willing to kill anyone who gets in the way.

HICNMBPA0309